DEADMAN CANYON

DEADMAN CANYON

LOUIS TRIMBLE

THORNDIKE
CHIVERS

This Large Print edition is published by Thorndike Press®, Waterville, Maine USA and by BBC Audiobooks Ltd, Bath, England.

Published in 2005 in the U.S. by arrangement with Golden West Literary Agency.

Published in 2006 in the U.K. by arrangement with Golden West Literary Agency.

U.S. Hardcover 0-7862-7589-8 (Western)
U.K. Hardcover 1-4056-3645-9 (Chivers Large Print)
U.K. Softcover 1-4056-3646-7 (Camden Large Print)

The text of this Large Print edition is unabridged.
Other aspects of the book may vary from the original edition.

Set in 16 pt. Plantin by Carleen Stearns.

Printed in the United States on permanent paper.

British Library Cataloguing-in-Publication Data available

Library of Congress Cataloging-in-Publication Data

Trimble, Louis, 1917–
    Deadman canyon / by Louis Trimble.
      p. cm. — (Thorndike Press large print Western)
    ISBN 0-7862-7589-8 (lg. print : hc : alk. paper)
    1. Drifters — Fiction. 2. Large type books.
    I. Title. II. Thorndike Press large print Western series.
    PS3539.R565D4 2005
    813'.54—dc22   2005002929

DEADMAN CANYON

I

Clay Belden came over the pass into the Wildhorse Valley shortly after sunset. He dropped out of the saddle and led his stocky dun pony out of sight of anyone who might be riding this way. Then he climbed up a big, honeycombed rock and positioned himself where he could watch without being seen.

He rolled a cigarette and smoked it slowly, looking over the valley while he waited for the October night to come. He couldn't see that much had changed in the five years he'd been away. Judge Lyles' Winged L spread with its fine, shiny white house and outbuildings and its neatly fenced pastures still took up the south half of the richly grassed valley. The dots of light marking the town to the north seemed no brighter nor more numerous than before.

Only Bick Damson's place would have

changed, Clay thought. And a shoulder of hill kept him from seeing that. He suppressed the quick anger the thought of Damson always brought him and stood up. The last of the evening light was fading to blackness over the Bitterroot Mountains to the west, and the stars were turning bright and hard and cold in the Montana sky. It was time to go.

Clay found the dun and led it back onto the wagon road. He mounted and gave the horse a light slap. "Keep to the middle and watch for chuckholes and you'll be all right, fellow," he murmured. "Now move along."

He let the dun choose its own pace down the steep switchbacks. He rode easily, a tall man with solid shoulders, his big-boned body drawn hard and lean from this last year of working in a Butte silver mine. His ears accustomed themselves to the steady clopping of the horse's hoofs and he listened beyond the sound, seeking any strange noise that might be out of rhythm with the night.

But he heard nothing, and when he came to the crossing with the hill road that ran along the high ground above the eastern edge of the valley, he stopped. Now the eagerness began to catch at him. His own land was just to the south and he felt the driving need to be on it once again. But memory of his talk with Judge Lyles when they had met in Helena two weeks back checked him. And once more he listened carefully to the night.

There was only the sound of the light breeze shaking the yellowing leaves of the aspens. Clay drew his rifle from the boot under his left leg and checked the load. He replaced the rifle and drew his handgun. He turned the cylinder so that the empty chamber was no longer under the firing pin. He holstered the gun and reined the dun to the right.

"Slow and easy along here," he whispered softly.

The trail was narrow and rough. As far as Clay knew, few people had used it since the time when a false silver strike had brought the first settlers into the valley. He had ridden it as a boy, both alone and when Tom Roddy had brought him here to teach him to read sign. Now he could feel the dun stumble over hussocks of grass and into weather-worn ruts.

They reached the branch trail that came up from Judge Lyles' Winged L, and from here on the ground was smoother. Clay pressed on, excitement drumming in him because now he was on his own land. But caution held him back because it was here that Judge Lyles had said he would find the trouble.

The trail forked a short distance on, the wider piece going straight ahead to the big bench fronting Deadman Canyon, the narrower twisting up the rocky ridges to the high country meadows. Clay reined the dun upslope, and rode with one hand on his gun.

The breeze picked up, stirring the aspen to loud whisperings. The tops of the pines began to sway and their lower branches rustled noisily against one another. Clay leaned forward to help the dun over the steep stretches and to urge it on to more open country where he could hear more clearly.

The flat crack of a rifle shot shattered the night air. Clay heard the bullet tick leather as it scored the cantle of his saddle. The dun whinnied and reared up, catching him off balance. The horse's twisting leap of fright lifted Clay out of the saddle and sent him crashing into the underbrush lining the trail.

His shoulder struck a rotting log. The punk wood broke his fall and he rolled behind the log and flattened himself against the darkness as the horse ran blindly alone one of the game tracks leading toward the rimrock above Deadman Canyon. Then the horse stopped abruptly, and Clay could hear only soft cracklings as the dun stirred about in dense brush.

He heard no movement at all to mark the position of the sniper.

He tried to hear over the sounds made by the night wind, but he could catch only his own ragged, pained breathing. Darkness danced in front of his eyes in bursts of bright color and he rubbed at them to clear his vision.

Hoofbeats sounded from above. Someone was riding along one of the game tracks, pushing a horse hard and dangerously fast. Clay drew his gun and rested it on top of the log in front of him. In a minute the rider should reach the trail. And if he turned toward the valley, he would be in sight just long enough for Clay to get in one shot.

Clay listened tensely as the hoofbeats grew louder. The sounds changed as the horse left the soft ground of the game track for the harder surface of the trail. Eagerness shook Clay as he realized the horse had turned downslope. He saw the dark blur of the horse's shape ahead to his left.

He took a deep breath to steady himself. In just seconds the sniper would be outlined against a patch of star-studded sky.

Th horse hammered on. It drew level with Clay. He let his breath out softly and fired. Too late he saw the empty saddle and realized he had been tricked into revealing his position.

A rifle blasted from across the trail. Pieces of log exploded in Clay's face. He had a quick glimpse of a solid chunk of wood just before it caught him a glancing blow on the chin.

The force of the blow sent him tumbling backwards. He rolled through a clump of wiry buckbrush and half fell, half slid over a sudden drop-off into a stand of scrub pine. He twisted noisily down through the maze of branches, landing on the ground on his knees.

He remained that way a moment, dazed but conscious of the sound of footsteps prowling past the log where he had been. He shook his head to clear it and squinted upward. He was acutely aware of all sensation now — the feel of blood running down his chin, the hammering of his heart in his ears, whispering night wind, the stalking footsteps coming closer.

He discovered that somehow he had kept

a grip on his gun. He caught his right wrist with his left hand and slowly, agonizingly lifted his arm until he had the muzzle of the gun pointed toward the edge of the drop-off above.

The footsteps grew hesitant, telling Clay that the sniper was unsure of Clay's exact position. Now the man could only feel his way forward, hoping for Clay to make another mistake and reveal himself again.

Clay's rough-hewn features twisted into a savage grin. He wouldn't be caught out twice the same way. He had played this grim game before — with claim jumpers in the Black Hills, with rustlers in Colorado, with Mexican *banditos* along the border. If it came to a war of nerves, he had his ammunition ready.

He tightened the grip of his fingers on his wrist as he felt his gun arm begin to tremble. The sounds grew louder above. The sniper was clumsy of foot, rustling the ground cover as he moved. A twig snapped dryly and Clay saw the bulk of a body against the night. His finger squeezed convulsively on the trigger as he steadied his gun arm again. Fire blossomed in the night. He heard a sharp curse of surprise and knew he had missed.

He fired again, blindly now, and a third

time. Footsteps hammered through the brush as the sniper broke and ran. Clay twisted to his right and sent a fourth shot screaming into the night. Then he dropped his arm and listened to the man run down the trail until he was swallowed by distance.

Clay crawled to his feet, cursing the wind for having drowned the man's first approach, and cursing himself for being so easily trapped. Then he realized that the sniper was on foot too. If he could find his horse first, Clay thought, he still might catch the man.

He whistled and heard an answering nicker from the dun. It was below and off to the left. Clay started in that direction, staggered as the full force of the bruising he had taken hit him, and went to his knees. He pulled himself up and fell again after two strides. He forced himself to his feet with an effort that brought the sweat breaking out over his body. He went on falling twice more before he found the dun standing nervously in a small clearing. With a final surge of effort, he pulled himself into the saddle and reined the horse back toward the trail.

Clay let the dun pick its way downslope. He clung to the horn, fighting the waves of blackness that battered him. When they reached the fork with the trail down to the Winged L, he stopped. He could hear a rider now, going fast along the hill road toward town. Clay sent the dun that way, pushing it as fast as his strength would allow.

They crossed the wagon road he had followed down over the pass, and now he could see the rider dimly ahead. Clay urged the tired dun to a faster pace, his one thought to catch the sniper and bring him, dead or alive, to Judge Lyles.

The hill road followed the rim of the valley, running straight most of its length but twisting here and there around an outcropping of rock. Halfway to town, Clay saw lights in a big, sprawling log house. That would be Bick Damson's new place, he guessed. Clay expected the rider to turn down Damson's trail. When he had left five years before, the last words he had heard were Damson's bellowed threats to kill him if he ever came back into the Wildhorse Country. And now, he thought, with Damson having struck it rich this past year, the man had the power to make that threat good.

But the rider kept straight on for town.

Clay felt the cold wind whipping strength back into him, and he dug his heels into the dun, forcing it to a pounding, frantic gallop. Once the sniper reached town, Clay knew he would be gone. There he could find half a dozen places to hide or to wait to finish what he had started back on Clay's mountainside.

The town lights swam closer. The rider raced past the first road leading to the fancy houses at this end of the small settlement. Then a bend in the road took him from view. Clay felt the dun stagger under him and he pulled it up reluctantly.

The sniper had had too great a head start. And Clay realized he lacked the strength to stalk the man through the streets and alleys where he might be hiding.

Clay reined downslope toward Judge Lyles' big white townhouse. It stood on a knoll with the valley and the mountains to the west spread before it. Clay turned the dun into the lane that led to the big yard between the house and the stable. He passed the little cottage where Tom Roddy lived. Once he had been the Winged L foreman, but since Clay had been a boy he had spent his time hunting the mountain cats that preyed on the judge's cattle. In exchange be received a pension and the small cottage at the rear of the big house.

Clay thought of stopping, but he wanted to speak to the judge before his strength gave out and he rode on. He pulled the dun to a halt by the rear door of the big house and half stepped, half fell from the saddle.

He caught his balance and walked slowly up the rear steps. He put a hand out and hit the door with his knuckles. He lifted his hand to knock again. The blackness closed down abruptly and he pitched forward. He fell on the splintery wood of the porch floor and lay still.

II

The smell of raw, cheap whiskey wrinkled Clay's nose. He lifted a hand feebly and opened his mouth to protest. He choked as a river of wet fire poured down his throat and exploded in his stomach. He opened his eyes and sat up.

"See," a voice said triumphantly. "I told you he wasn't bad hurt."

Clay looked into the bright eyes of Tom Roddy. He turned his head slowly and saw Tonia Lyles coming toward him worriedly. Roddy held out the whiskey bottle. Clay brushed it aside. The sight of Tonia was more warming right then than even Tom Roddy's particular brand of liquor.

She said, "Clay . . . ?"

"I'm fine, Tonia." Clay was surprised to see how little she had changed in five years. The promise of her childish prettiness had matured into beauty. She was still tall and slender and quick of movement, with fine features, her mouth full and warm, her dark eyes enormous in her oval-shaped face. But he saw a dignity that had been lacking before. And he found it hard to recall the sixteen-year-old tomboy who had sobbed so wildly when he left the valley.

She said, "Hello, Clay," and held out her hand.

He took it and held it to the point of awkwardness before he let loose. He looked around in embarrassment. He was on the sofa in the back parlor of Judge Lyles' house. Tom Roddy was still holding his whiskey bottle, grinning foolishly through his salt-and-pepper beard, looking no older and no less spry than Clay remembered him.

Roddy slapped his free hand on his skinny leg. "It's good to see you, boy. But we wasn't expecting you for a few more days. Leastwise that's how you wrote it in your last letter."

Clay sat a moment, not answering, trying to bring his thoughts back together. He rubbed a hand over his face, wincing when he touched the place where the block of wood had scraped his chin. He took away his hand and saw that there was no blood on it.

"Tonia washed you up good before you come to," the old man said. "She thought you was ready for Doc Fraley's hospital but I told her I seen you in worse shape when you got bucked off a bronco when you was a kid. I could say the same about her."

"You talk too much," Tonia said without heat. "I made some coffee. Will you bring it in, Tom?"

The old man strode off. Tonia looked broodingly at Clay and sat in a chair facing him. "What happened? And why did you come back earlier than you planned to?"

"Didn't your father tell you?" Clay asked. He looked around. "Where is the judge?"

Her lips compressed into a line of distaste. "He went to Helena on some kind of political business with Bick Damson. They won't be back until tomorrow." She gave him a quizzical look. "Didn't dad tell me what?"

Tom Roddy came in then, carrying a tray holding the coffee. He said, "About the trouble up on the summer graze, Tonia." He glanced at Clay. "I don't reckon he did tell her, seeing she's been over to the coast visiting up to a week or so ago."

20

Tonia stood up. "Stop talking in circles around me! What happened?" she demanded.

Clay picked up a cup and drank some of the hot coffee. He said, "Two weeks ago your dad and I met in Helena. I'd been writing him about the plan I had to turn that swamp and mountain land I own into a paying ranch. He wrote back and suggested we have a meeting."

He reached for his tobacco sack and began to shape a cigarette. "He agreed to the idea, all right, but there was a joker in the deck."

He struck a match and lit his cigarette. He sucked in smoke with deep satisfaction and leaned his head back tiredly. "You remember that three years ago I wrote and suggested the judge run some of his stock in the summer up in my mountain meadows. That way he could turn part of his valley pasture into new hayfields to grow extra winter feed and so increase his herd about thirty per cent."

"He did just that," Tom Roddy put in. "And it worked real good until this fall."

Tonia cried, "Why did I have to be away when things went wrong? What happened this fall?"

"The judge hired a drifter to go up in

the mountains and bring down the stock as usual," Tom Roddy said. "He always hires a drifter because the crew's mighty busy putting up hay. Well, this fellow rode up to the meadows, all right, but when he was bringing down his first gather someone knocked his hat off with a rifle bullet. He was the scairt type and he took off for town like a buckshot rabbit. And he wouldn't go back for anything."

"Someone really shot at him?" Tonia whispered.

"The judge didn't think so," Roddy said. "Figured he was just too lazy to work and looking for an excuse to quit. So the judge hired himself another man. That fellow lasted two days. Then he come down swearing he wasn't going to work no job where somebody kept shooting bullets in his coffee can. Leastwise not when it was hanging over the fire. He swore it happened two nights running."

"Didn't Roy Ponders do anything about it?" Tonia demanded.

"Sure he did," Tom Roddy said. "He deputized a bunch of men — Bick Damson and me and a bunch of others and we scoured that hillside. We didn't find nothing but fat shorthorns. Not even an empty rifle casing."

He gulped his coffee down and poured himself another cupful. "The judge was fit to be tied. With winter coming soon up in the mountains, he had to get that beef down to the valley. But he needed all his crew to finish the haying. And he couldn't get nobody to go up there and round up the stock. Not after them two drifters got through telling their story around. Nobody but me," he added.

He glared at them. "And don't try to tell me what the judge did — that I'm plumb too old for hazing steers out of the brush. I did just fine. I got me a whole day's gather in a rope corral up in the lowest meadow and was getting ready to bring 'em down when some coyote started shooting. Them cattle stampeded right through that rope and like to trample me to death before I could get out of the way. They all high-tailed it back into the brush where I'd got 'em."

"And you didn't see who did it?" Tonia asked.

"I didn't see a thing," Tom Roddy said. "It was getting dark then but I had time for a little hunting. I couldn't even find a foot-print. Whoever it was stayed on hard ground and picked up his shells after he got through his target practice." He finished the second cup of coffee. "I came and told the judge and he made me stay put down here. Just about that time he got Clay's letter and went off to Helena."

"That's the way the judge told it to me," Clay agreed.

"But who would do a thing like that?" Tonia demanded. "What reason could anyone have?"

"The judge thought it was a madman," Clay said. "He couldn't think of anybody who would want to keep him from getting his stock down from the mountains before snow fell." He looked inquiringly at Tom Roddy. The old man had always been a source of local gossip. If anybody had heard anything, he would be the one.

Roddy shook his head. "Nope," he said. "I'd like to think it was Bick Damson. But he's been trying to make friends with the judge since he got rich. Wants to go into politics."

Clay felt himself growing tired. He had put a in full day in the saddle and the bruising he had taken had sapped his remaining energy.

He said wearily, "At any rate, the judge pointed out that as long as someone was keeping people off my land, my plan for turning it into a paying ranch had no chance of working out. I said I'd come home as soon as I sold my claim in Butte and see what I could find. We planned it so the judge would let the word out that I would ride in day after tomorrow. That way we figured I could get here early and maybe surprise the sniper."

He leaned forward and put out his cigarette. "Only he did the surprising." He told the story briefly.

Roddy shook his head. "That's the first time the coyote ever tried to kill anybody. Before he just tried to scare 'em off."

"I was thinking that," Clay said soberly. "I remembered the threat Bick Damson made against me when I left town five years ago."

"That wasn't nothing to the show he's been putting on since the news got out you're coming home," Tom Roddy said. "The last few days, Damson's made it plain enough that quick as he sees you, he's running you right back out of the valley."

"That's ridiculous," Tonia cried. "Just because of a fight five years ago, he doesn't want Clay in Wildhorse?"

"Damson always was a proud man and a bully," Tom Roddy said. "When a nineteen-year-old boy whipped him in the town square in front of half the people and made him yell he was licked, it wasn't something he'd likely forget. Especially not now, when he aims to be a big man."

That would be the way of it, Clay thought. Damson couldn't stand to live in the same place with the one person who had publicly humiliated him.

"I stood up to Damson before," Clay said. "I can do it again."

"That was before he got rich," Tom Roddy said. "Now he's got the power to back up his threats."

Clay rose stiffly. "Tell me about it in the morning," he said. "Right now, all I want is a bed."

Roddy steered him to his cottage. Clay undressed and crawled under the covers of the extra bunk. He tried to find sleep but it wouldn't come. His mind kept turning to Bick Damson.

He thought of the unkempt, swaggering Damson he had known. A man who eked out whiskey and grubstake money doing odd jobs and who spent his spare time pecking away at a hole in the hillside behind his ramshackle cabin. Who boasted that someday he would find the rumored vein of silver that had brought the original settlers into the valley, but which had never been found.

Clay said, "Tell me about Damson, Tom."

The old man stirred in the darkness. "Last fall he struck that vein of silver he was always bragging about. And now he rides a palomino and dresses fancy and lives in a big new house."

"The judge told me all that," Clay said.

"Did the judge tell you that Damson hired himself some men? Two of 'em are supposed to be miners and one manages his business affairs." Roddy snorted. "If I ever saw hard-cases, them miners of Damson's is it."

Something in Roddy's voice made Clay ask, "And the third man?"

"Kemp Vanner," Roddy said. "He drifted in just about the time Damson hit that vein of silver. Funny about him — he's the one took to puffing Damson up in the first place. Seems like Vanner won't stop till Damson's big as they come, do just about anything to make that happen."

The name meant nothing to Clay. He stared up into the darkness as if there he might find the sleep he wanted so badly.

Tom Roddy said, "If Vanner thinks your being here will hurt Damson's chances of getting big, then he's the one to watch out for, boy."

"I've handled my share of men," Clay said.

"Sure, when you can see 'em coming," Roddy said. "But Vanner ain't that kind. When he's around, you got to watch front and back and both sides. And then you ain't too safe."

Clay barely heard him. He had finally found the sleep he needed.

III

Clay leaned against one of the wooden pillars holding up the roof over that piece of sidewalk belonging to the hotel. Now and then people spoke or waved to him, welcoming him home. He answered civilly enough but without moving from his position against the post.

Clay saw the stocky figure of Sheriff Roy Ponders moving purposefully down the wooden sidewalk toward him. He took out his sack of tobacco and began to shape a cigarette with slow, deliberate movements.

The sheriff came straight to where Clay stood and stopped in front of him. He was a heavy-set, middle-aged man with a stolid, almost bovine expression on his face. But the sharp, quick eyes had warned more than one would-be gunhand that the sheriff wasn't as stupid as he looked. Clay knew from experience that Roy Ponders could anticipate a man's moves in a way that made him seem like a mind reader.

"The stage isn't due for an hour yet, Clay," he said. There was no particular welcome in his voice.

"Maybe. I'm looking the town over," Clay said. "It's been a while since I saw it. Is there a law against that?"

Ponders' weathered cheeks flushed. "Don't push me just because you've got some kind of deal with Judge Lyles. I ran you out of town once. I can do it again."

Clay studied the sheriff with a deceptively casual look. He had been expecting this meeting since he had ridden into town from Tom Roddy's cottage earlier this morning. The sheriff had always been a fair man but he had never made any effort to conceal his dislike of the rough, easy-to-take offense kid that Clay had been. Nor had he made any effort to conceal his pleasure when Judge Lyles ordered him to run Clay out of town.

But that was five years ago, Clay thought. A man as fair as Ponders had been — tolerating Clay despite his dislike — should know that people changed, and boys grew up.

Clay said, "I didn't come here to start fighting, Sheriff. I came to settle down. All

I ask is the chance to do just that."

"You aren't waiting for the stage because you expect Judge Lyles to be on it," Ponders said accusingly.

"That's right," Clay answered. "I'm waiting for Bick Damson. If he means to back up his threats, I want him to get started. I've got work to do. I can't wait around wondering when I'm going to get a bullet in the back."

"Damson was just making a lot of noise with his talk," Ponders said. "You should remember that much about him."

Clay said quietly, "I was up on my land last night and someone tried to kill me."

Ponders snorted. "So you've run into the judge's mysterious sniper too! Even if there is one, he wasn't trying to kill you. Only frighten you off like he did the others."

"When a man rubs a bullet over my cantle, when he takes a second shot at me after I'm on the ground, when he stalks me through the brush, I figure he's trying to kill me," Clay said. "And if you want proof, Sheriff, you might ride up there and look for rifle casings. He didn't have time to pick them up this time. I chased him into town."

Ponders' expression was a mixture of disbelief and reluctant concern. "Without getting a look at him?"

"He had too big a head start. But go look, Sheriff. About halfway up the ridge to my first meadow."

"I might do just that," Ponders said. "After the stage gets in," he added pointedly. Then he shook his head. "Someone shoots at you and right away you want to fight Bick Damson. Why? Because he made a lot of noisy threats?"

"That piece of mountain to the south is my land," Clay said. "I'll fight anyone who tries to keep me off it." He straightened up. "If that man is Damson, then I'll fight him."

"If you find any proof that Damson or anyone else is up on your land, bring it to me," Ponders said flatly. "I'm the law here, not you." He glanced around. A few curious bystanders were watching from a distance but no one stood close enough to hear their talk.

"And don't go trying to stir up trouble by making threats against Damson — until you get some proof," the sheriff added.

"I can't make threats but he can? Is that it, Sheriff? Now Damson's got money and so he gets rights that I don't?"

Ponders' face turned brick-red under his heavy tan. "I played no favorites before. I'll play none now," he cried. "But you were a bigger trouble maker than any other two people in this town. Maybe you've changed. I'll feel a lot better when I know for sure."

"Five years can make a lot of changes," Clay said softly. "They made Damson rich." His gaze met the sheriff's steadily. "I hope they haven't changed you as much as it sounds, Sheriff. You were a good lawman."

The color faded from Ponders' face, leaving him white and shaking. He took a deep breath and then expelled it slowly. He turned and stalked away.

Tom Roddy drifted up from a doorway close by. "You was a little rough on him, boy."

"What does he expect me to do?" Clay demanded. "Wait until Damson gets in the first lick before I defend myself?"

"The first lick and maybe the second," Roddy agreed. "Roy Ponders is still a good lawman, but he's as human as the rest of us. And Bick Damson's rich and big and growing bigger. You keep that in mind."

Clay said stubbornly, "He made his threats to run me out of the valley as soon as he saw me. All right, I'm going to be right here, where he can't miss seeing me."

"You're just as feisty as you ever was,"

Roddy said. "And you don't pay much more attention to advice than you did before. I told you Damson has three men working for him. It won't do no good to brace him. He'll just huff and puff and make a lot of noise. And while he's doing it, Kemp Vanner can come up from behind and run a knife into you."

"If this Vanner's around, I wish he'd start trying," Clay said.

"Oh, he's around," Roddy answered. "He rode into town early this morning. He's been sitting over in the Cattlemen's Bar ever since. And don't think he ain't got a tight eye on you right now."

Clay could see genuine concern in the old man's sharp blue eyes. And when Roddy got a burr under his saddle this way, Clay knew it meant something.

He glanced across the street to the far side of the town square and the front of the Cattlemen's Bar. He could see that the half-curtain covering the lower part of the front window was pulled back a few inches, just enough to give a man watching a good view of the spot where Clay stood.

"I'll just save the sheriff some worry," Clay said. "Maybe I can get this settled before Damson ever gets here."

He stepped into the street and strode toward the Cattlemen's Bar. Roddy stood watching him for a moment and then followed. He touched the hunting knife he always wore at his belt, as if to make sure it was still where it belonged.

It was that hour between breakfast and noonday dinner when most men still hadn't worked up a thirst and the Cattlemen's was quiet and almost empty. When Clay stepped inside, he saw only four men — a balding bartender lazily polishing the big mirror back of his bar, two seedy looking drifters playing a desultory game of cards at a table by the alley door, and a neat looking man sitting by the curtained front window.

Clay looked hard at the man by the window, the one who was Kemp Vanner. A dozen feet from him, Clay stopped and let his eyes take in all there was to see — a small, slender man, city dressed in a dark suit and flat-heeled boots. Thin leather riding gloves and a black, hard-crowned hat lay on the table beside a half-empty cup of coffee.

"Vanner?" Clay said.

"That's right," Vanner's voice was light. He had a round, bald-looking face and dark eyes with oddly cold flecks of laughter in them. "I've been watching you prop up

35

that post in front of the hotel," he said. He sounded as if he found this amusing.

"I'm waiting for your boss to come in on the stage," Clay said. He made it a challenge.

Vanner merely shook his head, then stood up and carried his coffee cup to the bar. The bartender stopped polishing his mirror and hurried to refill the cup from a graniteware pot. Vanner made no offer to pay, but carried the cup back to the table and sat down. His movements had an easy grace that reminded Clay of a stalking mountain cat.

Clay noticed with interest that Vanner wore no gun under his neat-fitting coat. Vanner turned an unblinking stare on Clay. And suddenly, without the kind of reason that he could put into words, Clay knew that this man hated him with a viciousness that made him deadlier than a dozen shouting, bullying Bick Damsons could ever be.

Vanner's voice lost its lightness. "You're wasting everybody's time, Belden. You aren't wanted in this country. My advice is for you to ride before Mr. Damson gets back."

"Are those *Mister* Damson's orders?" Clay said mockingly.

36

"If you really need an answer, here it is," Vanner said. His voice was soft but it cut with the cold deadliness of a winter wind. "You have a bad reputation as a troublemaker. Mr. Damson has too many important matters with which to concern himself to bother worrying about you. Part of my job is to see that he isn't bothered. *This* warning is mine."

Clay took a step forward, his fists doubled up. Then he relaxed them, realizing the futility of anger at Vanner. The man was physically too small for Clay to strike. He said, "And this is my warning, Vanner. Last night I was shot on my own land. I was holding Damson to account for that. But he isn't the kind to hide in the dark and shoot a man in the back. I think maybe you are that kind. The next time I'm sniped at, I'll take a ride down into the valley and maybe do some shooting for myself."

Vanner said contemptuously, "I wouldn't waste my time crawling around that pile of rocks you own."

He picked up his coffee cup and turned his head away.

Clay said, "To make sure, let's go check your bootprints against the fresh ones somebody left up on my pile of rocks last night, little man."

Color surged into Vanner's cheeks. His hand shook, slopping coffee over the side of the cup. He made an obvious effort to control himself, but when he spoke his voice was tight and highpitched.

"You're leaving Wildhorse, Belden — now."

He nodded his head toward the rear of the saloon. Then with studied indifference he drank down his coffee.

Clay threw quick glance toward the table by the alley door. The two seedy drifters who sat there were watching him carefully. The nearest man had his gun out and was making a pretense of wiping the metal with a rag.

A scraping noise turned Clay toward the bar. The bartender had a shotgun lying across the bar so that the barrel pointed directly at Clay. He was rubbing the palm of his hand over the dully gleaming wood of the gunstock, humming softly as he worked.

Clay moved his eyes from the bartender to the drifters and back to Vanner. A surge of wild anger ran through him and started his hand down for his gun. He pulled himself up short as he remembered Vanner was apparently unarmed. The triumph in Vanner's eyes died.

Clay took a half step forward and a half

step sideways. He stopped, holding his hands well away from his sides.

He said casually, "You don't run this town, Vanner." His eyes traveled to the pair of drifters by the rear door. "And you never will with an army like those two." He took another step, again half forward and half sideways. And now he was directly between Vanner and the barkeep.

Clay saw the soft, slow opening of the rear door. He said quickly, "Keep that door shut, Tom!"

The eyes of every man swung toward the door. Clay dropped to one knee, beneath the line of fire of the shotgun. As he moved, he slapped his hand down, drawing his .44. He had a quick glimpse of the bartender looking back toward him and reaching for the trigger of his shotgun. He saw the shocked expression on the man's face as he realized that Vanner and not Clay was in his sights now.

Clay looked toward the drifters. The one with the gun was sitting very still as he stared into the muzzle of Clay's .44. "Go ahead and shoot, friend," Clay said softly. "Let's see how fast you can squeeze that trigger."

The man let the barrel of his gun drop slowly. "I didn't hire out for no gunplay," he said to Vanner.

Clay heard Vanner stir but he kept his eyes on the drifters. The door began to inch open again and Clay called, "All right, Tom." His voice turned crisp. "Now, you two, throw your guns out to the middle of the room."

Two guns thudded to the floor. The drifters got to their feet and began to back toward the far corner of the saloon. The door swung open and Tom Roddy stepped in, a wide grin splitting his whiskered face. The grin disappeared abruptly.

"Clay, watch out!"

Clay twisted around in time to see Vanner lift his hard-crowned hat from the table with one hand. The other hand held a small gun that had been concealed under the hat.

Clay's own gun was still aimed at the rear of the room. He knew he had underestimated the smaller man. He stared helplessly, watching Vanner's finger whiten on the trigger of his hide-out gun.

IV

A woman's voice shattered the taut silence in the barroom. "Kemp, no!"

Both Clay and Vanner looked up to the top of the stairs that rose at the far end of the bar. Clay stared in amazement as he recognized the woman who stood on the landing. It was Molly Doane. She was wearing a gold dress of the kind he associated with dance-hall women. She had become well filled out for her small size. She wore her blond hair swept up on top of her head so the round prettiness of her face was accentuated. Elaborate diamond earrings sparkled on each ear.

He found it hard to connect this sleek, well-fed woman with the Molly Doane he remembered. He had last seen her fighting Bick Damson's drunken maulings in the alley behind this very saloon. She had been pinched from hunger then, a still-proud

41

girl who hated the hand-me-downs the town ladies gave her for cleaning their houses or tending their children.

Molly walked down the stairs with her head held high. She looked scathingly at the two drifters. "Get out of here," she ordered. The pair broke and ran for the door. Molly stepped between Clay and Vanner and stopped.

"Both of you, put those guns away," she said. She turned to Clay as he got up off his knees and holstered his gun. Her hands came out, capturing his. He saw warmth spring into her eyes and he knew that in some ways she had not changed. Because he had been one of the few in town who treated her as a person and not as "that poor daughter of Jake Doane," she had been grateful to him. Uncomfortably he remembered that once she had mistaken her gratitude for love, despite the fact he had shown no more than friendliness toward her.

She had a ghost of that affection on her face now as she murmured, "It's good to see you, Clay. You're looking fine."

"So are you, Molly," he said. "Real good." His eyes went past her shoulder to where Vanner still sat. Clay saw the man's hatred standing naked on his face and thought, *He's in love with Molly Doane!* A glimmering of understanding about Vanner's hatred of him appeared in Clay's mind. Molly would have chattered about him to Vanner. Clay couldn't know what Molly had said, but he knew it was enough to make Vanner think of Clay as a man to hate.

Clay slipped his hands free. "I owe you a favor now, Molly," he said.

"Let's just call it part payment for all the things you did for me," she answered.

Vanner's chair scraped back. He strode across the room and up the stairs, carrying his hat in his hand. He stopped on the landing and looked down. "When you're through with Belden, come up here!" It was an order.

His head swiveled toward Clay. "You've had my warning, Belden." Then Vanner turned and disappeared up the stairs.

"Does he try to run you too?" Clay asked, looking down at Molly.

Her cheeks turned pink. "I work for him," she said. She stepped back, letting her hands fall to her sides. "I guess I should say I work for Bick Damson really. He owns the Cattlemen's now, you know. But Kemp is the one who comes here and watches over the business."

That explained the bartender's backing Vanner, Clay thought. He glanced at the bar. There was no sign of the shotgun. There was no sign of the barkeep, either. There was only Tom Roddy, pouring himself a drink from a bottle of whiskey. He tossed it down and carefully laid his money on the bar.

Molly said suddenly, "Kemp has been good to me, Clay." Her eyes swept down the expensive dress she wore and lingered on the diamond rings glittering on her small hands. "Awfully good," she murmured.

"I'm glad for you," Clay said. He stood awkwardly, not knowing what to say next.

A shout rose from the street outside. Tom Roddy trotted to the front window and squinted out. "Stage coming!"

Clay said hurriedly, "Thanks again, Molly. I'll see you sometime soon."

He ran for the door with Roddy at his heels. He heard Molly's despairing cry, "No, Clay, don't be foolish! Leave Bick Damson alone, please!" And then he was outside.

Clay saw the stage coming into town with its usual flourish, raising a cloud of dust as it careened around the square to make its swinging stop in front of the

44

hotel. He was on the wooden sidewalk before the concord had stopped rocking on its braces.

Roddy pulled Clay's arm. "Ain't you seen enough trouble for one day, boy?"

"I've seen the beginning," Clay said flatly. "I want to see the end — now."

The stage door swung open and Bick Damson stepped out. He was a heavy man, thick through the body and legs. He was dressed in a dark suit and fine boots with silver threads chased through their soft leather tops. As he stepped to the street, his coat fell open to show the silvered gunbelt he wore around his waist. Clay wasn't fooled by the fancy clothes. Underneath them he could see the same man he had beaten into the dirt five years ago. The fleshy features still shouted their arrogance; the big, solid body still moved with a bully's swagger.

Clay jerked his arm from Roddy's grasp and stepped down from the sidewalk. "I hear you wanted to see me, Damson."

Damson had been facing the stage with one hand out as if to help someone to the ground. His hand dropped down and he swung around to Clay. "By God!" he whispered. "Belden!"

Clay could feel the crowd that had gathered stiffen in anticipation. Someone called nervously, "Better get the sheriff, quick!"

"He's coming," another voice called back.

Clay kept his eyes on Damson. "Are you going to run me out now like you said, or are you going to wait for Roy Ponders' help?" he demanded tauntingly.

A savage grin twisted Damson's heavy mouth. He took one step toward Clay and then another. Suddenly he broke his stride and lunged forward, reaching for Clay with his huge hands.

Clay tried to side-step Damson's rush, but the crowd had pressed in too close. He bounced off someone's shoulder and half fell toward Damson. He felt the strong hands catch him around the waist.

"I've been waiting a long time for this!" Damson grunted. He jerked Clay up against him and began to squeeze with his thick arms.

Clay could feel Damson's thumbs digging into his backbone. He thought, *Someone taught him some tricks since the last time we fought.* He tried to surge back, to break that rib-crushing grip, to get away from the pressure of those paralyzing thumbs. His heart began to hammer as his breath gushed out of him and a numbness spread through his muscles.

With a final effort, he twisted sideways and broke Damson's hold. Damson brought up a knee, driving it for Clay's groin as he staggered away. Clay turned, taking the punishing blow on the point of his hip. He fell into the crowd again, but this time when he bounced back, he had his balance.

He rocked on his toes, watching Damson step slowly toward him. Beyond Damson's triumphant face, he saw Judge Lyles standing in the stagecoach door. There was no expression on the long, austere face, no hint of partisanship in the blue eyes. The judge was just waiting.

Clay sucked air into his lungs and stepped temptingly toward Damson, letting both hands hang at his sides. The numbness had left his muscles but he knew that if Damson got him in a grip once more, it would be all over.

Damson broke his stride and rushed. Clay danced away and drove a hard fist into Damson's mouth. Damson stopped and shook his head, spitting blood. He made a thick sound deep in his throat and lashed out at Clay with a wild fist.

He's lost his temper, Clay thought. Deliberately, he waited for Damson to lift his guard and swing again. Then he stepped in close and hit Damson twice, twisting his fists in an effort to cut the skin over Damson's eyes.

Damson raised both hands and reached for Clay as he stepped back. The judge said sharply, "Here comes Roy Ponders!"

Damson stopped, shaking his head. Clay let his arms fall to his sides. He stood breathing deeply while Damson took out a fancy handkerchief and wiped blood from the corner of his swollen lower lip.

Damson put away the handkerchief and, without a word, drove himself against the crowd, splitting it apart. He stalked onto the sidewalk and into the lobby of the hotel.

Roy Ponders came around the side of the stage, a foolish look on his face. "You're early," he said angrily to the stage driver. He looked apologetically at Judge Lyles. "I was across town on business or I'd have been here sooner."

The judge merely nodded and stepped down from the stage door. Ponders turned on Clay. "I warned you, Belden."

"Did you warn Damson too?" Clay asked softly.

The sheriff reddened and put a hand out

to take Clay's arm. Judge Lyles moved forward. "Be careful, boy," he warned. "To arrest a man, you have to have something to charge him with."

Ponders' hand fell back. "I thought . . ." he began. He compressed his lips, cutting off the flow of words.

Judge Lyles nodded to Clay. "I think we have something to talk about." He was a tall man and his eyes moved easily above the crowd. "And I see Tonia came with the rig. Shall we ride to the house? It should be about dinnertime." He spoke easily, as if nothing out of the ordinary had happened.

Clay felt the curious stares of the crowd and sensed some of them were hostile. A lot of people remembered him as a wild kid who'd been run out of town five years ago. Like the sheriff, they expected the worst from him.

"I could use something to eat," Clay said.

"I'll fetch your horse to the house," Tom Roddy called. He gave Clay a heavy wink and cocked his head at the sheriff, who was walking away with as much dignity as he could manage.

Clay walked with the judge to the edge of the square where Tonia was waiting with a small rig. She leaned out and kissed her father as he climbed up beside her. She slid over on the seat, leaving the reins for Clay. He could feel the warmth of her close to him with the three of them squeezed together. He heard her murmur, "You should know better than to let Bick Damson get his arms around you that way."

Clay clacked the team into motion.

Judge Lyles snorted. "A lady isn't supposed to watch a fight, let alone enjoy one."

"I didn't enjoy it until Clay started winning," she retorted. She laughed, the husky, tomboyish laugh Clay remembered from their childhood. "I'm sorry Roy Ponders stopped it. I think it's about time Bick Damson had another beating."

The judge said, "If it was only another fight, that would be fine. But you know it won't be. Bick Damson won't stand being reminded of what Clay once did to him. Not now."

"I thought you two were friends, Judge," Clay said quietly.

"If you mean that my traveling to Helena on business with him makes us friends, then I am," the judge said. "If you mean do I want him as a guest in my house, the answer is, not yet. He's neither friend nor enemy. I can't afford to have either one, Clay. I'm still a judge and I'm supposed to be impartial. I'll give Damson the same chance I would anyone else to make himself into a good citizen. But that doesn't stop me from expressing an opinion on something that everyone in town knows already."

"You aren't on the bench now, Dad," Tonia said. "Can't you admit that Bick Damson started that fight?"

"No," the judge answered. "Clay provoked him into making the first move."

The judge's voice carried no accusation, but Clay had no illusions about the way the older man felt. At their meeting in Helena, he had made it plain that he was reserving judgment until he was serious about coming home and settling down. But, Clay thought, the judge had put enough trust in him to ask for his help.

Nothing more was said on the subject until they finished dinner. Tonia left the men to their coffee and cigars. Then the judge said, "Did you get up to your place last night, Clay?"

Clay told him in a few words what had happened. When he finished, Tom Roddy said, "Judge, that's the first time the sniper ever tried to do more than scare anybody off. But this sounds like he was out for blood."

"I thought that myself," the judge admitted. He glanced at Clay. "You didn't get a clear look at him?"

"No, sir," Clay admitted. "But I have an idea who might have hired him." He recounted his meeting with Kemp Vanner.

"I warned Clay about that coyote," Tom Roddy said angrily. "If it hadn't been for Molly Doane, Vanner would have used that hide-out gun of his for sure." He bit into the end of his cigar. "And me standing there armed with nothing but a belt knife," he said disgustedly. "A man my age ought to know better than to run around naked when Vanner and his kind are in town."

The judge frowned. "I'm surprised Vanner would resort to using a gun," he said. "Before, he's always been very careful not to do anything to call attention to himself — especially the law's attention."

"It wouldn't help much if he was arrested," Clay said frankly. "Not the way Roy Ponders is favoring Bick Damson."

The judge's lips thinned out. "Don't get the wrong idea," he snapped. "Roy Ponders is still a good, fair lawman. But he has a peaceful town here and he wants to keep

52

it that way in the few years left to him before he retires. And you can't blame him for expecting you to cause trouble," he added pointedly.

"All I ask is an even chance," Clay said. He waved a hand, brushing the matter aside. "But that's neither here nor there right now, Judge. The problem is to get those cattle of yours down to the valley before snow comes in the mountains."

The judge said grudgingly, "I could pull my crew away from haying. The sniper wouldn't bother that many men."

"We made an agreement, sir," Clay pointed out. "Part of that agreement was for me to round up your stock and get them back to the home ranch." He pushed back his chair and stood up.

"You need a little help?" Tom Roddy asked hopefully.

Clay shook his bead. "Not up there. But I could use a pair of ears in town — to find out what Damson and Vanner are doing."

"I can tell you what Vanner will be doing," Tom Roddy said flatly. "You pretty well tipped your hand to him today. He'll be figuring a way to get you killed — if he has to hire a half-dozen snipers for the job."

"You have no proof that Vanner is behind the snipings," the judge said stiffly.

"I got no proof, Judge," Roddy agreed, "but I get a pretty strong feeling every time I see him."

Clay moved toward the door. "If there is any proof, I'll bring it to you," he told the judge.

"If you stay alive long enough," Roddy said gloomily.

The judge said quickly, "Let me send my crew up, Clay. There's no need for you to risk yourself this way."

"No, sir," Clay said flatly. "I want the man who shot at me last night. And I want to know why he's been keeping people off my land."

"Just remember that he has the advantage of surprise," the judge warned. "You'll be in the open and he won't."

"I thought of that," Clay admitted. He opened the door and went out.

V

Clay rode into town and bought a week's supplies. He was tying his pack behind his saddle when he saw Roy Ponders coming stiffly down the sidewalk. Clay finished his tying and then rolled a cigarette while he waited for the sheriff to reach him.

Ponders stopped on the edge of the sidewalk and studied the full pack. "Leaving us, Clay?"

Despite what Judge Lyles had said, Clay didn't feel sure enough of the sheriff to confide in him. He said warily, "I have business to attend to."

Ponders pushed out his lower lip thoughtfully. He said in a reluctant voice, "I've been told you didn't start that fight with Damson today."

Clay swung into the saddle. "That's one way of looking at it, Sheriff. Damson rushed me as soon as he got off the stage."

He looked down, meeting Ponders' gaze steadily. "But I didn't give him much choice, did I? And that's another way of looking at it. Take your choice."

Ponders flushed. He said, "Either way, Damson didn't lick you. But you're leaving." His voice was sharp with suspicion.

Clay said with quick anger, "We all have work to do, Sheriff. I believe in getting mine done as quick as possible."

The flush on Ponders' face deepened. "I warned you before about riding me."

Clay leaned forward. "I own a piece of land in that valley, Sheriff, and every year I've mailed in my tax money for it. I always thought that gave me as much right to protection as the next man."

"If you need protection, you'll get it," Ponders answered.

"You were quick enough to try to keep Damson and me from fighting," Clay said. "But I haven't noticed you riding into the mountains to check on the sniper who tried to kill me last night."

The color drained from Ponders' cheeks, leaving them a dirt white under their tan. "If there was a sniper," he said angrily.

"You could have tried to find out before he had a chance to get back up there and brush out any signs he left," Clay retorted.

Clay saw the anger glitter in Roy Ponders' eyes. It faded slowly. "Maybe I made a mistake," Ponders said. His gaze moved beyond Clay as if he were commenting on something removed from the subject at hand. He turned away suddenly and walked stiffly on down the sidewalk toward the hotel.

Clay started the dun down the street. He noticed little as he rode. His mind well out into the valley before he became aware of his surroundings.

He looked back as some one called his name. He saw Tonia coming toward him on a sleek sorrel. She rode at a wild gallop, but she sat the horse as if she were part of it.

Clay reined in and waited, watching in admiration. The wind had whipped color into her cheeks and a glow into her eyes. For a moment he was content to stare in wonder at the beautiful woman she had become.

She was dressed in a split riding skirt and a colorful shirt. She wore a wide-brimmed hat crammed down over her dark hair. Her clothes hadn't changed in five years but she filled them out quite differently. He kept his eyes on her as she came abreast and slowed her horse to a walk.

She glanced at the pack behind his saddle. "Dad told me you were going to bring his stock down," she said. "But you're hoping to find the sniper too, aren't you?"

"That's right," Clay said.

"And you think Bick Damson or that man Vanner is behind the sniper. You're hoping to prove that." Her voice was stiff.

Clay gave her a puzzled look. "What are you trying to say, Tonia?"

"I don't want you to go up there," she said simply.

Clay could only stare at her in surprise. She spoke quickly now, the words rushing out of her. "Things have changed here since I was visiting on the coast," she said. "I can't explain it but everybody is different — even dad and Roy Ponders. It's that man Vanner. He's using Bick Damson and his money to get control of the valley."

"He might want to," Clay said dryly, "but he's got a long way to go yet. If there was any sign of that, your father would stop it."

"That's what I mean," Tonia cried. "It seems so obvious — Damson going into politics and buying up the Cattlemen's Bar and the mortgages on a lot of property from the Helena bank. And nobody seems concerned. They just say it's good business on Damson's part."

She waved a hand around her. "If there's a drought or cattle prices drop, he'll own half this end of the valley. Most of the little ranchers on the west side won't be their own bosses anymore. They'll work for Bick Damson."

"You've been listening to Tom Roddy," Clay said.

"What of it?" she demanded. "Tom can see what's going on, and he's not afraid to speak up."

"I don't like it any better than you and Tom do," Clay told her. "But what's that got to do with my not going into the mountains?"

"Don't you see?" she cried. "Damson can't afford to have you around — not after the threats he's made. And Vanner can't afford it either. Because if you did manage to make a success of your ranch, then you and dad together would be bigger than Damson could ever hope to be."

Clay gave her a puzzled look. "You're afraid of Damson's power but you don't want me to try to fight him. What kind of sense does that make?"

Tonia flushed. "I've waited for you for five years," she whispered. "People laughed at me and told me you'd never come back. But I knew you would, and I kept on waiting." She turned her eyes away from him. "I could stand waiting again — if I knew you would come back. But I couldn't stand it if there was — wasn't anyone to wait for."

"What do you want me to do?" he asked. "Turn tail and run? Leave the valley to Damson and Vanner?"

"You wouldn't do that," she said in a low, controlled voice. "Even if you hadn't promised to bring dad's cattle down to the valley, you wouldn't stay away from the mountains."

"Why should I?" he demanded. "It's my land. I have a right to be on it."

She swung toward him, her eyes blazing with sudden anger. "Is that why you're going? Because it's your land and you want to live on it? Or are you trying to make a fool of Bick Damson? Trying to dare him to do something to you? Dad told me how you plan to make your place into a paying ranch. But you'd risk that — you'd risk everything — just to prove that Damson and Vanner can't run you out of the valley! It's your stupid pride that makes you go back up there now!"

She raked her heels across the sorrel's

flanks and sent it flying down the road toward the Winged L. Clay made no effort to follow. Her sudden attack had caught him by surprise and left him confused.

A woman in love just made no sense sometimes, he decided as he jogged the dun along. With a man it was different. He had to learn to put his feelings aside when there was work to be done. Clay was not a man who expressed his emotions easily, and he knew he had not let Tonia know how empty these past five years had been.

But, he thought, there was more behind Tonia's outburst than her fear for him. He was sure she'd had more reasons than she'd given for not wanting him to go up into the mountains. For the first time since he'd known her, Clay had the feeling she had not been completely frank with him. And that was so unlike Tonia that it made no sense at all. Yet the more he turned over her words, the more sure he was that he was right.

He worried the problem past Bick Damson's land with its new fencing and elaborate house and on to the north edge of the Winged L. The road turned here, starting east toward its climb over the pass. Clay saw two men working in a hayfield bordering the road, and he recognized Pete

Apley, the foreman of Judge Lyles' ranch, and Bert Coniff, one of the hands who had hired on the year before Clay left the valley.

He waved to them and then glanced back along the road. He caught a glimpse of Tonia and her sorrel racing up the lane leading to the Winged L headquarters; then she disappeared behind the big white house. Clay turned his dun east and started toward the pass.

He saw a pair of riders moving fast along the hill road. They reached the crossing with the main road and went on past, toward Clay's land. When he came to the crossing, he slowed the dun and reached down, loosening his rifle in the boot under his left thigh.

He saw the riders again as he rounded a bend in the trail. They sat their horses in the middle of the road, looking his way, clearly waiting for him.

Damson's men, Clay thought angrily. They had seen him in the valley and had been ordered to ride this way to head him off. The trick was typical of Bick Damson. Vanner would have been more subtle. But not Damson. Money wouldn't have changed his belief that, by throwing enough force against a man, you could break him.

As Clay drew close, the men moved their horses so that they blocked the trail. Clay pulled the dun up and looked the pair over slowly.

They were strangers to him. The smaller one was short and wiry, with narrow, bright eyes and sharp features; the other was as big as Bick Damson but soft looking, with a dull, almost empty expression on his heavy face.

The small one moved his horse closer to Clay. "You're Belden?" he demanded in a thin, reedy voice.

"That's right," Clay said.

"I'm Abe Marnie," the small man said. "And this here is Ben Pike. We work for Mr. Damson." He grinned at Clay, showing a badly broken set of teeth.

Clay looked quietly at him, saying nothing.

"We figured you might need a little help getting out of the valley," Marnie said. His grin broadened. "What with snipers in the mountains and all."

Clay said slowly, distinctly, "Go tell Damson that if he wants to fight me, to crawl out of his hole and do it himself."

He lifted the reins as if to move the dun along. He saw eager desire for action spring into Marnie's face and he had a quick glimpse of Pike making a clumsy move toward the gun on his hip. Clay jerked the reins suddenly, wheeling the dun around and ramming it against Marnie's horse, pinning the small man's leg down.

Marnie cursed shrilly and leaned back to reach for his gun. Clay caught the front of his coat with both hands. He urged the dun back and then jerked Marnie out of the saddle. He pressured the dun with his knees, urging it forward so that Marnie's horse stumbled back toward Pike.

Pike had his gun up now but he couldn't shoot with Marnie hanging between him and Clay. The dun drove forward as Clay raked a heel across its flank. Pike tried to back his horse away but he moved too slowly. Clay threw Marnie at him and Pike raised his hands and dropped his gun in an effort to keep the smaller man from knocking him out of the saddle.

Marnie hit the ground on his side, rolled and staggered to his feet. He reached for his gun and stopped only when Clay pulled his rifle from the boot.

Marnie stared at the rifle and then his head swiveled slowly around toward his partner. Pike had both hands on his saddlehorn. His eyes were on Clay's rifle, and his expression said that he wasn't interested in going after his gun lying on the ground.

Clay said quietly, "Throw your gun down, Marnie."

Marnie looked back at Clay, his eyes squinted as if he was trying to find some advantage in this for himself. Then he pulled his gun and let it fall to the road. He stepped back toward Pike's horse.

Clay rode the dun to Marnie's horse and caught the reins. He looked at Pike. "Climb down," he ordered.

"It's my horse!" Pike objected in a thick voice.

Marnie turned a scathing look on him. "Do what the man says. Don't you know when you're whipped?"

Pike left the saddle and Marnie led the horse to Clay and tossed him the reins. "I never argue with another man's gun," Marnie said dryly. His broken-toothed grin showed again. "But you're wasting your time, Belden. Like Mr. Vanner would say, you're just postponing the inevitable."

Clay studied Marnie silently. He figured there wasn't much to Ben Pike but blubber, but Abe Marnie was a different story. The way Clay read Marnie was grim. With someone to lead him, Marnie was a man who could cause serious trouble.

Clay turned the horses in the direction of town and lashed his reins across their rumps. Pike yelled in dismay as both animals kicked up their heels and galloped down the road.

Clay said, "Now start walking."

Marnie stepped toward his gun and then away as Clay waggled his rifle. Marnie said, "You've had all the warnings you're going to get, Belden."

"So has Damson," Clay said quietly. "Now move."

VI

The shadows were growing long and the air was turning cool with the threat of coming night when Clay rode up the meadow trail to the spot where he had been ambushed the night before.

He wasted little time looking for signs the sniper had left. A few quick looks showed him that the man had been back and brushed out his tracks.

In making his final check, he walked to the edge of the drop-off where he had shot at the sniper. He glanced around, expecting to find nothing. Suddenly he bent down and studied the ground with close attention. The sniper had overlooked one clear heelprint. The print showed a heel that had been worn away on the inside so that the outer edge made the deeper impression. In the center of the print there was a small puncture, as if a nail was working loose in the heel itself.

Clay straightened up with a grunt. It wasn't much to go on, but it was tangible. It was something he could show Roy Ponders if he ever had the chance.

He glanced toward the west and saw that the last of the sun was sliding over the distant Bitterroots. He hurried back to the dun and rode it down to the big bench that fronted the mouth of Deadman Canyon. He made his camp where a high shoulder of rock jutted from the steep hillside marking the north edge of the bench. He built his fire in front of a shallow overhang formed where the shoulder of rock met the hillside. Here he was protected on three sides, so that the sniper could approach only across the open bench.

Clay half expected an attack, but the night remained quiet. In the morning, work pushed the problem of the sniper to the back of his mind. Clay's plan was to avoid wasting time by driving the judge's stock down to the valley day by day. Instead, he decided to corral them until he had a fair-sized gather and then move them onto Winged L graze in a bunch.

With this in mind, he threw a brush fence across the small opening leading into Deadman Canyon. The canyon itself was long and narrow, well grassed and well watered, and enclosed by barren rock walls that rose sheer from the floor higher than a man could look without cricking his neck.

The canyon had not been a place Clay liked to come as a boy. The towering rock walls kept out the sun most of the day, making it gloomy. And he had never ridden near it without remembering how the canyon had got its name. In the early days a silver prospector had died there when a snowslide caught him at the back of the canyon and buried him alive.

Clay glanced toward the far end of the draw now as he worked to set up his brush fence. A great scar on the cliff face and a tumble of boulders at the end of the grass floor told him that flood and storm had been at work here since his last visit some seven or eight years before.

He reminded himself to ride to the end of the canyon soon and see if the rockslide might not have uncovered one of the old watercourses that honeycombed these mountains. He had found a number of them not far away when he was a boy — long smooth tunnels burrowed out of the rocky cliffs by long departed rivers. They had fascinated him then, but he had never ventured far into them because the air inside always had the rank smell of bears clinging to it.

The brush fence finished to his satisfaction, Clay rode into the high country to see how many of the judge's cattle he could spot easily. The judge had told him a hundred head were driven up in early summer. Checking the largest of the meadows, Clay counted only forty beeves. That meant the rest would be scattered, in the brush and higher up the mountains.

Clay squinted at the sky. It was bright blue and the sun still held a certain warmth. But he could feel the chill of coming winter whenever he stepped into the shade, and he knew he had no time to waste if he was to find all the cows and get them safely into the valley before the first snow came up here.

He spent the first days moving down those cattle grazing in the meadows. They were ornery and stubborn after a summer spent in the mountains, and none of them wanted to leave. Clay found that working alone he could only shag a few head at a time down the steep trails to the bench, and he spent the better part of three days before he had forty head corralled in Deadman Canyon.

While he worked, he kept his eyes open

to see if the country was as he remembered it, and if it would fit into his idea of turning this mountainside into a paying spread. His plan was to run a small herd of his own in these meadows during the summer and keep them in feed lots during the winter. The problem that had always stopped him whenever he'd considered this before was how to get the large amounts of hay he would need for winter feed.

Then a few years back he had found the answer while helping on a fall roundup in Colorado. There, a large swampy area had been drained and made into hay meadow. Clay's own hundred acres of swamp had never been anything but a nuisance — all cattails and bogland. Now he realized that if he cut his ditches right, he could not only drain the area, but he could catch all the water from the springs that caused the swamp.

The one flaw in the plan was the fact that by taking over the meadows for himself, he would hurt the Winged L. Clay knew the judge had put a lot of money into extra beef and haying machinery so he could take advantage of Clay's offer to use his mountain grazing land. In Helena he and the judge had talked about what could be done with the extra stock Winged L would have once there was no longer any place to graze it.

The judge had suggested that he sell the beeves even though it would mean taking a heavy loss on them. But if he did that, he would still have a lot of extra hay and haying machinery on his hands. Clay pointed this out, but the judge waved the objection aside. If the judge believed in a man, he had always been ready to make personal sacrifices to help that man out.

Now, as Clay stared down into the valley, he saw the solution to this final problem. The slope of the land was just right for him to channel his swamp drainage over to the judge's dry south section. Under irrigation, it would provide all the graze the judge needed to keep his extra cattle.

Excitement ran through Clay as he studied this new plan carefully. He even took time to ride into the valley and trace a possible channel from the swamp to the judge's dry section. It would work! He curbed an impulse to ride to town and tell the judge about it. After he got the stock all rounded up would be time enough since nothing could be done until spring anyway.

That problem taken care of, Clay turned his attention back to his own meadows. He saw that they were even better than he remembered. In a few places the trails between one meadow and another were little more than animal tracks snaking up steep mountainsides or edging along the lips of canyons. But in every case, Clay noted, he could blast out fair trails with a few sticks of dynamite.

Finally he worked his way to the high grass lands, a sprawled prairie, boggy right up to the end of the summer when it usually dried up just in time to catch the first heavy frosts. He found a dozen head of Winged L beef grazing on the browning grass, and he started them down to the lower country.

The trail from the high grasslands dropped steeply down a mountainside, narrowed to a cut across the face of a cliff rising out of a deep-bottomed gorge, and then broadened to enter a pine-fringed meadow.

Clay shagged the bawling steers onto the narrow part of the trail and reined in the dun. He watched the steers as they plunged in panic across the cliff face to the safety of the meadow. There, in typical ornery cow fashion, they calmed down and began to crop grass as if the idea of coming down here had been their own all along.

Clay studied the rough surface of the trail and the sheer drop alongside it. The fact that he had not been bothered by the sniper since coming up here bothered him. He had seen no one after sending Marnie and Pike running home with their tails between their legs.

A delayed attack wasn't Bick Damson's usual way of operating. He had never waited in his life that Clay could remember, but always bulled in, arrogantly sure of his own strength. And Damson wasn't a man to stand by and let the story of how Clay had handled his men get around. Even if Damson wasn't behind the sniper, Clay reasoned, he would have tried by now to get back at Clay for what he'd done to Marnie and Pike.

Unless Vanner had talked Damson into waiting. Clay considered this possibility. Vanner was a man who would seldom rush hurriedly into anything. He would bide his time, looking for the approach that would let him do the most damage with the least risk.

Clay had the uneasy feeling that moment wasn't far off. Each night he built a small signal fire on the rock above his camp, letting the judge and Tom Roddy know that he was all right. By now, the meaning of that fire would have circulated around town, and everyone would know Bick Damson hadn't made good on his threat to run Clay out of the valley. And once the townspeople started to laugh at Damson, something would have to give. Clay didn't think that even a man like Kemp Vanner could hold Damson back once the big man realized he was being made a public joke.

Clay squeezed his eyes into a squint at the glare of the bright October day and raked a careful glance over the jumble of hills on the far side of the gorge. His gaze lingered on a deadfall made from the roots and branches of a huge pine uprooted by some previous winter storm. Had he seen a stirring there or was this waiting and wondering making him jumpy?

He looked away and back again. There was no sign of movement near the deadfall. The air hung still and quiet in the sunshine, without even a hint of a breeze. Clay grunted.

"Another few days of this and I'll be seeing snipers in every shadow," he told the dun. He gave it a slap. "Let's get those cows down where they belong."

The dun nickered softly and moved out onto the narrow trail. Clay rode with one hand on the butt of his rifle. He felt a little

75

foolish, but the uneasy feeling stuck in his craw and he couldn't cough it free.

He was nearly to the meadow when a rifle shot hammered through the still, cool air. Clay felt the whip of the bullet tug at the crown of his hat. He threw himself forward over the dun's neck and lashed back with his heels. The dun surged forward as a second shot sent chips of rock flying just behind its kicking hoofs.

The trees fringing the meadow cut off the sun abruptly. Clay straightened up and reined the dun to a halt. He pulled his rifle from the boot and dropped to the ground. He hurried back to the first tree at the end of the trail. From here he could see the far side of the gorge. He stepped into the open and raked the distant slope with three quick shots. The echo of his firing boiled through the rocks and then faded away. The air hung silent and golden in the sunlight, mocking him emptily.

Clay stepped behind the protection of the tree and stared at the hillside. Nothing stirred. There was no hint at all that a man bent on killing him had been there a few moments before. Angrily, Clay strode back to the dun and mounted.

He left the cattle grazing and started down the trail leading to the meadow just below. A short distance along the trail, he reined to the right and forced the dun down a ridge that would bring them to the far side of the gorge where the sniper had hidden. He pushed the dun upslope until he decided he'd ridden as close as he dared to the deadfall. Then he left the saddle and went on foot.

He made his way surely, drawing on childhood memories for the fastest and easiest route to the point he wanted to reach. He approached the top of the slope and stopped. He dropped to his belly and slid cautiously over a hump of rock.

Now he looked down on the deadfall. There was no sign of movement, no sign of life. Clay climbed to his feet and worked his way from one barren upthrust of rock to the next until he reached the side of the deadfall. He squatted down, studying the ground carefully. It was hard packed but he could make out a long shallow gouge, as if someone had crawled along here, dragging the edge of his boot across the dirt.

Clay followed the gouge. It made a twisting, turning path that carried him into the center of the deadfall. Here soil-packed roots made a room, the roof high enough for Clay to kneel under without having to bend his head. Directly in front of him was a narrow opening where dirt had been pushed from between entangled roots. He squatted down and peered through the opening. The narrow trail he had ridden on was directly across from this spot. He looked down, hoping to find an empty cartridge case, but as usual the sniper had cleaned up after himself carefully.

Clay backed out of the deadfall and looked around speculatively. The man had gone westward, he decided. A narrow fold of land ran from the far end of the deadfall to a stand of stunted trees. By crawling west along this fold to the trees, the sniper could have got away without being seen from across the gorge.

Clay followed the fold until it reached the stand of trees. The forest duff had been disturbed, and he felt he was on the right track. He hurried along the upward pitch of land and almost missed the heelprint outlined sharply in a spot of moist dirt. He stopped abruptly and went to his knees. It was the same sign he had found before — a worn heelprint with a small puncture in the center.

Now he was sure he was following the sniper and he straightened up and moved on. He came out of the pines on top of a ridge. He saw where the sniper's horse had been tied to a bush and his eyes picked out a nearby deer track that clearly showed the marks of fresh hoofprints.

Clay trotted along the ridge until he came to a point above that where he'd left the dun. He plunged down through a tangle of brush to the horse. He mounted and rode back eastward. As he remembered this chopped up land, the trails the sniper had to use led down into the valley only after making a wide sweep to avoid the high cliffs that surrounded the south side of Deadman Canyon. If he was right, he could follow the regular trails down to the bench and take a shortcut from there that might put him in the valley before the sniper could reach it.

He held the dun back until they were over the steepest pitches. Then he urged it to a faster pace until they were going at a hard gallop as they reached the level trail leading to the bench. Clay reined in at the far side of the bench, trying to recall the exact location of the shortcut he remembered. He turned to his right and rode downslope until a thick stand of timber blocked him. He backed the dun a short distance and circled the trees until he saw the faint, narrow track he remembered.

Now he moved swiftly again, following

the faint track as it twisted dangerously down through thick brush and then across a barren stretch and finally joined with another, equally faint trail.

From here he could see a corner of his swampland and the judge's dry south section. He looked down at the trail and elation surged in him. The surface of the ground showed the fresh tracks of the sniper's horse clearly. They pointed uphill, telling Clay the man had come this way.

He felt the dun stir under him and he leaned forward, listening. He could hear the sounds of someone riding hard, coming from well above him. Clay smiled with soft savagery. Now it was his turn.

VII

He backed the dun into a screen of trees and returned to the trail on foot. He crossed to the other side and climbed a low mound. He squatted down, keeping the hump of the mound between himself and the upper side of the trail.

He breathed softly, curbing his eagerness as he listened to the hoofbeats coming nearer. Now they were just a short distance above him. He lifted his head. The horseman was just a few feet away, riding with his head down and his hat pulled low. He was pushing his horse at a dangerous pace on the narrow, faint surface of the rough trail.

Clay drew his handgun and sent a shot in front of the racing horse. He called loudly, "You there! Hold it!"

The man jerked at the reins and lifted his head. He twisted toward Clay. Surprise froze Clay as he stared up at the slack features of Bert Coniff, one of the Winged L's top hands.

Clay saw Coniff slap his hand down to his side and come up with his gun. Clay's inclination was to shoot Coniff out of the saddle. Common sense kept him from doing it. He wanted the man alive. He dropped his gun and dove for Coniff's leg. Coniff shouted as he lost his balance and slid out of the saddle.

Clay let his weight ride Coniff to the ground. He felt a shod hoof tick his hat as Coniff's horse took fright and dashed down toward the valley.

Clay felt Coniff twist frantically under him in an effort to bring up his gun. He caught Coniff's wrist in his fingers and squeezed down. Coniff cried out as the gun dropped to the dirt. Clay let loose of Coniff's wrist and drove his fist into the slack-featured face, feeling cartilage and bone give under the angry force of his blow. Coniff threw up a knee in an agonized effort to shake Clay off him. Clay swung his fist again, burying it in the softness of Coniff's stomach. Coniff gagged with pain and sagged back.

Clay crawled to his feet and picked up Coniff's gun. Coniff rolled over and came to his knees. He stayed that way, his head hanging, while he gagged, gasping for air.

Clay got his own gun and put it in his holster. He turned back to Coniff. "On your feet," he said.

Coniff lifted his head slowly. Blood ran from his nose down over his mouth. He wiped it away with the back of his sleeve and stared at Clay. His eyes mirrored fright and pain.

Clay said softly, "Who hired you, Bert?"

Coniff shook his head slowly like an injured dog and got awkwardly to his feet. "I don't know what you're talking about," he said thickly. "What's the idea of jumping a man like that. You gone crazy?"

Clay hesitated, for the first time wondering if he might have made a mistake. He hadn't known Bert Coniff from before he left the valley, but he remembered a pleasant enough man who did his work well with no more than the usual cowhand's complaining. He could find no reason why a man like that, with a good job as long as he cared for it, would take the risks necessary to kill a man from ambush.

Clay said, "Step back in that soft spot over there, Bert, and I'll let you know if I'm crazy or not."

Coniff gaped at him. Clay took a step forward and Coniff backed up. Clay said, "Stop right there. All right, now move away."

Coniff wiped his sleeve across his face again and did as he was told. Clay looked down at the bootprints he had made in the soft dirt. One heel left a mark that was an exact match for the worn ones Clay had seen before.

"Look for yourself," Clay said softly. "You left that heelprint with the little puncture in the middle back up by the deadfall today. And you left another one just like it near where you tried to shoot me the other night. Take a good look, Bert. That worn-down heel is going to put a rope around your neck."

"You're crazy!" Coniff blurted. "Why would I shoot at you? I was up here hunting deer."

Anger drove Clay forward. He grabbed Coniff by the shirt front. "I want to know who hired you!" he yelled.

Coniff's slack features went white with fear. He lifted his hands and batted at Clay's wrist. "Leave me alone," he cried. "You got no call to treat a man this way. I ain't armed and you are. What chance have I got?"

Clay let loose of Coniff and stepped back. "If that's the only thing bothering you, we'll fix it," he said. He tossed Coniff's gun aside and unbuckled his own belt. He dropped it on the ground.

He started toward Coniff at a slow, deliberate walk. Coniff held his ground for a moment and then turned. He broke into a shambling run down the trail.

Clay took a long stride and launched himself in a tackle. He caught Coniff around the waist and swung him to the ground. Coniff twisted about and began to flail wildly with his fists. Clay slapped his arms aside and pinned them to the trail. But anger turned to disgust as he stared down into the fearridden features. This was a far cry from the Bert Coniff he had known, and he wondered what had happened to turn what had once been a man into this craven animal.

Clay said slowly, "Let's start all over, Bert. Who hired you to keep people off my land? Damson? Did Bick Damson's money get to you?"

Coniff shook his head.

Clay cocked a fist. Coniff said, "It won't do you no good to beat me up. I ain't got nothing to say. If you think I been shooting at you, run me down to the jail and bring charges." Confidence surged into his voice as he talked. "Sure, that's it. You got a case against me, bring a charge."

Clay thought Coniff's eagerness a little overdone. He was too anxious to put himself in Roy Ponders' hands.

But there was nothing else he could do, Clay realized. Even if he had thought it would make Coniff talk, Clay knew beating the man would only make him despise himself. This was a job for the law now — Roy Ponders and Judge Lyles.

Clay could imagine how the judge would feel when he saw how one of his trusted hands had betrayed him. Clay sighed. Then he got up and pulled Coniff roughly to his feet. He pushed the man up the trail. "Let's go," he said angrily.

Coniff seemed to realize that he was no longer in danger of a beating. "You're wasting your time," he said. "I was up here to get me a deer and you can't prove otherwise."

Clay stopped to put on his gun and belt. "We'll let the law decide," he answered. He herded Coniff ahead of him to where the dun waited. He climbed into the saddle. "Now start walking."

Coniff turned and stepped back onto the trail. He glanced back at Clay and then broke into a run, seeking to climb the low bank on the far side of the trail and reach the protection of the timber.

Clay urged the dun out of the trees, untying his rope from his saddlehorn as he rode. He fashioned a rope and threw it just as Coniff scrambled to the top of the bank. The rope settled around Coniff's body, pinning his arms to his sides. The force of his run pulled the loop taut. He snapped upright then went over backwards, tumbling down the bank and sprawling on the trail.

He surged to his feet and tried to run again. Clay brought the duo alongside him and took a few more turns about Coniff with the rope. He tied the free end to his saddlehorn.

"Walk or get dragged," Clay said flatly. "It makes no difference to me."

"I ain't going to walk all the way to town," Coniff cried. "It's five miles."

"Maybe your horse waited for you down the trail," Clay said dryly. He kicked the dun into motion. Coniff waited until the rope stretched taut, then he started reluctantly forward.

They found his horse at the foot of the slope, eating rank grass growing along the edge of Clay's swampland. Clay pulled

Coniff's rifle from the boot and then let Coniff work his way into the saddle.

"You try any fancy tricks and you'll learn what a roped steer feels like," Clay said. "Start riding."

Coniff squirmed his arms around in front of his body and managed to get the reins into his hands. He started his horse forward sullenly.

"You make a man feel like dirt," he complained.

Clay said only, "Just head for town."

He glanced around as they came into the valley. He could see some of the Winged L men haying in a distant pasture, but they were too far away to see what was going on.

They neared the new fencing which marked the edge of Damson's land. Clay saw the bulky figure of Ben Pike some distance ahead. Pike was working on a corner fence post with a hammer and a bag of staples, but he stopped quickly enough when he saw Clay and Coniff coming steadily down the road.

He took a long, gape-mouthed look and then broke for his horse. Clay reached down for his rifle. He let it fall back into the boot as he saw Pike rein his horse around and head for Damson's big house.

Trouble, Clay thought. Pike would have gone to tell Damson or Vanner what had happened.

Clay urged the dun to more speed. Coniff tried to hold his horse back, and Clay swung around to him. "Don't count on Damson helping you," he said. "If you're working for him and he gets the idea you might talk, he'll shoot you first and think up a reason later."

Coniff kicked frantically at his horse, sending it galloping up the road.

VIII

Bick Damson drove his big palomino at top speed the three miles from his place into town. He followed the hill road, making a wide swing so that he came into the alley behind the Cattlemen's Bar from the far side of town. He rode the horse into a small barn and got hurriedly out of the saddle. He strode across the alley and into the rear door of the Cattlemen's.

He was in a narrow hallway with the door to the barroom straight ahead and a flight of stairs leading upward on his left. He climbed the stairs two at a time and entered a door at the top.

The room was fitted out as a combination parlor and office. Molly Doane was seated behind a desk, making entries in a ledger. She looked up coldly as Damson shut the door behind him.

"This is my room," she said. "You've

been told to come in here only when you're invited. You have a room of your own. Use it."

"Where's Vanner?" he demanded. "I got to talk to him."

"Downstairs eating his supper," she answered. She went back to her work. "Now get out of here."

"Don't get so high and mighty with me," Damson shouted. "It's my money that put you here. Go tell Vanner I want him and be quick about it!"

She paid no attention to him and he strode angrily to the desk, one hand lifted. Molly opened a desk drawer and brought out a small gun. Only then did she lift her head and look at Damson.

He stopped abruptly. "By God," he whispered. "I think you'd like a reason for shooting me." He took a backward step. "Put that thing away and listen to me. All hell's going to bust loose pretty soon. Get Vanner up here."

Molly stood up. "Go to your own room and I'll bring him." She looked around at the expensive furniture. "I don't want you in here, dirtying up the only decent things I ever owned."

Damson backed toward the door. "Someday Vanner'll get tired of you. Then you'll be glad to have me around. And anyone else you can get."

Fear touched Molly Doane's eyes briefly. She turned hurriedly away from Damson's gaze. "Just get out," she said.

Damson jerked open the door and strode down the hall to a room that had been set aside for him. He hurried to a sideboard and poured himself a big drink of whiskey. He downed it and took the bottle and glass to a chair. He poured a second drink and gulped it angrily. Then he slumped back, staring impatiently at the door.

Vanner came into the room quietly. He glanced at Damson and took a chair near him. "You were told to keep out of Molly's room," he said.

"Whose money bought this place for her?" Damson demanded. "Who —" He waved the question aside. "Listen," he said. "Clay Belden's got Bert Coniff hog-tied and he's bringing him into town. I told you we shouldn't wait to get rid of Belden."

He poured himself a third drink and swallowed it jerkily. "Coniff'll talk and then what?" He pushed himself forward in the chair, glaring at Vanner. "You're always bragging about how many brains you got. How you made me rich and you're going to fix it so one of these days I'll own the whole valley. All right, if you're so smart, figure out what we do right now."

"I've thought of a number of solutions if Coniff should get caught," Vanner said coolly. "The simplest one is to kill Coniff before he gets a chance to talk."

"He's probably told everything he knows to Belden already," Damson said. "I say get rid of Belden and Coniff both."

"Don't be a fool," Vanner said acidly. "It's too late to do anything to Belden. It has been too late ever since you got drunk and made those threats against him. Why do you think I ordered Coniff to wait until he had a chance to drive Belden and his horse off a cliff and make his death look like an accident? Any other way and you'd be the first man everyone would suspect. You or I. We can't afford that."

Damson poured himself another drink. "You think we can afford to have Coniff shoot off his mouth?" he demanded.

"How much does Coniff know?" Vanner asked quietly. "Now put that bottle down. We have work to do."

Damson glared at him with drunken stubbornness. "*We* got work to do," he mimicked. "You don't do nothing but sit around and think of ways for me and the boys to wear ourselves out."

"And where would you be if it weren't for my thinking?" Vanner said.

He got up and took the bottle away from Damson. He said, "Everything that's been done to make you a big man, I thought up." His voice cut mercilessly at Damson. "The few times you've acted on your own, you got into trouble. You threatened Belden — behind his back. You told Coniff to shoot him the first night he came back into the valley. You sent Marnie and Pike to chase him away. All you've accomplished is to build up evidence that not even the sheriff will ignore one of these days."

"He sure ain't going to ignore what Bert Coniff has to say," Damson grunted.

"Anything Coniff has told Belden, we can claim is a lie," Vanner answered quietly. "Our job is to keep Coniff from talking to the judge or Ponders. Bert doesn't know why we have to keep Belden from settling on that land of his, so he can't hurt us by saying anything about that."

"Sure" Damson jeered. "Go tell Roy Ponders you want to talk to Coniff real quick."

"You're the one who's going to talk to

him," Vanner said in his quiet way. "After it gets dark, you go to the window of his cell. I'll make sure the sheriff isn't in his office. When he goes to the hotel for his dinner, I'll hold him there someway. You find out just how much Coniff has said. Then promise we'll have him out in a couple of days — *if* he keeps his mouth shut."

A glimmer of understanding touched Damson's eyes. "Then tonight one of the boys shoots him?"

"Not tonight," Vanner said quickly. "Tomorrow. It's Saturday and I can arrange for it better then. A dozen men have been drifting in these past few days. By tomorrow, they'll all be here. So leave things to me. Go eat something to soak up that whiskey inside you."

Damson lurched out of the chair. "That takes care of Coniff and the town, maybe, but Belden is still running around loose. He's no fool. One of these days he's going to figure out that we got to get him out of the valley for good."

"I've already planned a way to get rid of Belden," Vanner said.

Damson walked slowly and carefully to the door. "You better make it quick," he warned. "And remember, we ain't got the sheriff in our hip pocket just because he don't like Belden."

"I know what kind of man Roy Ponders is," Vanner answered shortly. "I know just how far we can count on his dislike of Belden and on his desire to keep a peaceful town here. You let me worry about such things."

"I don't like it," Damson complained. "I say let's get rid of Coniff tonight and Belden too."

"No," Vanner said flatly. "Somebody has to take the blame for killing Coniff." He stood and smiled his cold, thin smile. "I've already prepared for the possibility someone would catch Coniff and bring him in to jail."

Damson made a snorting sound. "You mean that story you started around town that the judge was worried about going broke if Belden came back and started his ranch?"

"Exactly," Vanner said.

Damson shook his head. "Ain't nobody going to believe that," he said decisively. "Everyone in town knows the judge'd give his right arm away to help someone he likes. And he likes Belden. Always did," he added in a surly voice. "Besides, how will a rumor like that help us?"

"It's very simple," Vanner explained with soft patience. "We've got a lot of people thinking we're all right just because I made you lend money to the little ranchers and because we bought the Cattlemen's and turned it into a place where a man could come and get good food and liquor cheap and find an honest game of cards." He paused and added, "Not to mention the pretty girls Molly brings in to dance with the men on Saturday nights. That means these people are on our side right now."

He stood thoughtfully and then said, "Now all I have to do is make the rumors a little stronger — get the story started that the judge is really worried that Belden is going to be a success. People will figure out for themselves that the judge paid Coniff — his own top hand — to get rid of Belden."

"What difference does that make?" Damson shouted. "Coniff didn't do it. Belden ain't dead!"

"No, but Coniff will be by tomorrow night. And who'll get the blame for killing him?"

"Belden," Damson said hopefully.

"Not Belden," Vanner answered. "He won't be around to be accused of killing anybody. But Tom Roddy will."

"Roddy!" Damson cried. "Why waste time on an old fool like that?"

"Because Roddy pokes his nose into everything," Vanner said. "And ever since Belden came back, he's been poking deeper. If he gets even a little smell of what we're doing, he'll guess the rest. I've been meaning to take care of him for a long time. Now I'm going to do it."

Damson snorted. "You're crazy! Nobody in Wildhorse would ever believe Roddy killed anybody."

"They will when I start some more stories moving," Vanner said confidently. "Who does Coniff work for? Judge Lyles. Everybody knows that. And everybody has heard the story we started the day Belden came back — that the judge will be bankrupt if he loses the use of all that good, grazing land Belden owns."

"You're still crazy," Damson said. "Sure everybody's heard the story. But that don't mean they believe it."

"Plenty of them do," Vanner said. "What do you think the dealers and waiters and the dancing girls do here? They listen to the talk. And they tell me what they hear."

He shook his head at Damson. "I've told you before that I use my head. I don't make a move until I'm sure. And right now

I'm sure of the temper of the local people who come in here. It won't take much more talk to light a fuse under them. Figure it out for yourself. Who does Tom Roddy think is the greatest man alive? Judge Lyles! Roddy likes Belden, yes. But he'll protect the judge's interests first."

Damson said slowly, "You're going to fix it to look like Roddy shot Coniff to keep him from telling Belden it was the judge hired him to do the sniping?"

"I'm going to do more than that," Vanner said. "By the time I'm finished, you won't own just a part of the valley. You'll own the whole of it — and the town as well."

He stepped closer to Damson and lowered his voice. "Why do you think I've had men coming in here these last few days? By tomorrow night we'll have a dozen top gunhands working for us. If the locals won't start a vigilante committee to get rid of Roddy, then the new men will. I have it all arranged."

"I don't like this bringing in hardcases," Damson grumbled. "What happens if they get out of hand?"

"I can control men!" Vanner said flatly. He looked coldly at Damson. "Have you a better idea? Can you think of another way to protect all the work we've done so far? Maybe you're satisfied to take what you've got now and let Belden have the rest?"

"No, by God!" Damson shouted. "If we don't do nothing else, I want Belden out of the way."

"I told you that I'm taking care of him too," Vanner said. "You send Marnie and Pike in to see me. I have a job for them."

He smiled his thin, cold smile. "There's one thing you can count on — by moonrise tomorrow night, Belden will be dead."

IX

Clay pushed Bert Coniff through the jail-house door and into the sheriff's small office. Roy Ponders rose from his neat desk and stared in bewilderment from Clay to Coniff.

"Here's your sniper," Clay said quietly. He unwound the rope from Coniff's body.

Coniff rubbed his hands over his arms. "That's a lie!" he cried. His confidence seemed to have come back now that he was no longer alone with Clay. "I was up hunting me a deer and —"

"I have proof," Clay interrupted. He told Ponders about the heelprints he'd found.

"That don't mean nothing!" Coniff said.

"And this time he won't get a chance to rub out the signs he left," Clay finished. "You come up to the mountain tomorrow and bring Bert's right boot along. We'll see how much it means."

Ponders still stood quietly, his expression troubled. "For your sake, I hope you're right," he told Clay. "Bringing false charges can be mighty serious." He frowned. "But for the judge's sake —" He broke off and shook his head. "Bert Coniff's been with the Winged L for better than five years," he went on. "It just doesn't make any sense."

Clay nodded, understanding what was going on in the sheriff's mind. He said, "I've been thinking of that all the way in here. And the only answer I could find is that Bick Damson's money got to Bert."

"Damson isn't a killer," Ponders protested. "He wants you out of the valley, but that doesn't mean he'd try to kill you."

Clay took off his hat and dropped in on the sheriff's desk. He poked a finger at the bullet burn on the crown. "This is how close Bert came today," he said. He told Ponders about meeting Marnie and Pike a few days before.

"How else do you add it up, Sheriff?" he demanded when he'd finished.

Ponders said, "I haven't got evidence enough yet to add up anything." He looked at Coniff who had been standing sullenly since his outburst. "What about it, Bert? Did Damson hire you?"

"I got nothing to say," Coniff replied. "You ain't about to believe anything but what Belden here tells you."

Ponders flushed. "It isn't my job to believe or disbelieve yet," he said stiffly. "It's my job to find out the truth."

Coniff grunted surlily. Clay said, "Maybe he'll talk to the judge. I stopped by his house but there was no one around."

"He and Tonia and Tom Roddy all went out to the ranch," the sheriff explained. He frowned again. "If this proof you claim to have holds up, the judge isn't going to be a very happy man. But he has to be told — and soon. He'll want to see Bert."

"I'll stop off at the ranch on my way back to camp," Clay said. He glanced out the window at the shadows lengthening along the street. "But I don't imagine he'll come in tonight."

"If he does, I'll be around," Ponders said. "Otherwise I'll wait until he comes in tomorrow before going to your place."

"I'll tell him," Clay said. He stepped back as Ponders came forward and motioned Coniff to follow him. The two cells opened directly onto the office. Both were empty and Ponders put Coniff in the one looking directly toward his desk.

Clay felt a sense of relief as he watched the sheriff go efficiently about locking up Coniff and then return to his desk to take down the particulars of Clay's charge. His uneasiness at the thought that Ponders might favor Coniff dissolved. The sheriff was acting again like the kind of man Clay remembered — doing his work without letting his personal prejudices interfere. Clay thought that the judge might well be right and Ponders had warned Clay only out of concern for keeping his town peaceful.

He would know more certainly tomorrow, after he saw how Ponders acted in the face of the proof he had to offer.

The sheriff finished writing down Clay's charge. "All right," he said. "I'll be along tomorrow. Meantime, keep out of Bick Damson's way." He glanced toward the cell where Coniff sat dejectedly on a bunk. "I've got enough trouble as it is," he added.

"As long as Damson doesn't bother me, I won't bother him," Clay said flatly. "I told you that before, Sheriff. But if you're thinking of my tangling with that pair of gunslingers he calls hired hands, remember they were trying to keep me off my own land."

"I won't argue the point," Ponders said

with a touch of weariness in his voice. "I'm just telling you to avoid trouble. If Damson is behind what's been happening, I'll find out about it. If he isn't I'll find that out too."

"Who else wants me out of the valley?" Clay demanded.

"The sniper was driving people off your land before you ever came back home," Ponders reminded him. "Think about that when you start laying the blame on Bick Damson."

Clay picked up his hat and settled it on his head. "I've been thinking about it," he admitted. He started for the door. "And I've been remembering that the sniper shot only to scare people — not to kill them. Until I came back."

He opened the door. "I'll put Bert's horse in the livery, Sheriff."

Ponders nodded. Clay went out into the cool shadows of evening. A small crowd of curious boys had gathered when he paraded Coniff through town, but there were none about now. It was suppertime and they had found something more important to attend to, Clay thought with a faint smile.

His stomach said it was suppertime for him too. After he took Coniff's horse to the livery stable, he rode slowly toward the Cattlemen's Bar, thinking about getting his meal there. He saw no sign of the fancy palomino tied outside to indicate that Damson might be around.

Ponders had cautioned him about tangling with Damson, but he hadn't said anything about Kemp Vanner, and he hadn't said anything about Molly Doane.

And, Clay admitted to himself, as much as anything he wanted to go into the Cattlemen's on the chance he might be able to talk to Molly. He had thought a good deal about her during the long days in the saddle. He wanted to know more about her relationship with Vanner and Damson. And he had the idea she might be able to answer some of the questions that bothered him.

He swung the dun toward the hitchrail in front of the saloon. He dismounted and crossed the sidewalk. Pushing open the doors, he stepped into warmth and noise.

Th big barroom was fairly well filled with men eating or drinking or just listening to Molly Doane. She and a piano player were on a raised platform at the rear of the room, and she was singing in a thin but pleasant voice.

Clay's eyes moved past her to a table where Bick Damson sat with his head down over a plate of food. He looked up suddenly, as if he'd felt Clay's gaze. Even from where he stood, Clay could see that Damson was drunk and he tensed himself for possible trouble.

Molly picked up her song again as Damson settled back and returned to his food, ignoring Clay.

Clay walked quietly to an empty table on his left and sat down. Molly finished her song. Scattered applause sprang up. "Don't let the faro dealer go to sleep, boys," she called with forced gaiety. She stepped down from the platform and made her way to Clay.

"You shouldn't have come in here," she said anxiously. "Damson's drunk and he's upset about something."

"I came for a meal, not a fight," Clay said. He looked at her closely, noticing the little puckers of worry at the corners of her mouth, the tiredness around her eyes.

"And to say hello better than I did the other day," he added.

Molly glanced toward the stairs by the bar. They were empty and she turned back to Clay. "Kemp is upstairs," she said suddenly. "He — he wouldn't like my talking to you."

"How much does it matter what Vanner

likes or doesn't like?" Clay demanded.

"I work for him — in a way," she said. She added, "It's the only really good job I ever had in my life." Her eyes were pleading as she stared down into Clay's face. Beneath the pleading he saw again the warmth he had noticed the other time they had met.

"I'm not trying to spoil anything for you, Molly," Clay said. "Did I ever?"

"No," she answered fiercely. "You were about the only person in this town who didn't though. You were the only person who ever treated me like a human being."

"Until Kemp Vanner came along," Clay said. He saw color flood her cheeks and added, "Just because Vanner and I don't get along doesn't mean we can't still be friends, Molly."

She was looking toward the stairs again. She said abruptly, "I'll get you some dinner, Clay," and hurried away, holding up the edge of her striking, close-fitting gold gown.

Clay watched her go and then looked toward the end of the bar. Vanner was coming down the stairs, moving in that neat, graceful way of his. He showed no sign of being aware of Clay's presence, but when he reached the foot of the stairs, he stopped Molly and spoke to her briefly. Then he came directly to Clay's table.

Clay turned his eyes toward Damson's table. He was gone. Clay decided that Damson must have left while he talked to Molly. Uneasiness stirred inside of Clay. That wasn't like Damson — to walk out on a chance for a fight.

He pushed the thought of Damson aside as Vanner came quietly up to the table. Vanner pulled out a chair and sat down without being invited. He said pleasantly, "Your dinner will be along presently."

Underneath the pleasantness, Clay sensed coldness. He studied the smaller man, noting again the empty features, the deliberate, meaningless smile, the ice lying in the dark eyes.

Vanner said, "I hear you claim you caught the mysterious sniper." His voice was light.

"News travels fast," Clay said dryly. "Did you also hear I think you hired Coniff?"

Vanner shook his head easily. "I hadn't heard," he answered. "But I'm not surprised." His voice tightened almost imperceptibly. "Don't make the mistake of confusing issues, Belden. Mr. Damson doesn't want you around, but that doesn't mean he's trying to kill you." Vanner's smile was touched with contempt. "When he gets ready to run you out of the valley, he'll do it his way. With his fists."

Clay's uneasiness increased. Vanner was being too obvious. There was something behind these words, something more than just the bare threat against Clay himself.

"He sent his hired gunhands to run me out," Clay said. He watched Vanner carefully.

Vanner shook his head. "That was their own idea. They thought they were helping the boss. Let's say they were a little too eager."

A heavy-set man with an apron tied under his armpits came up to the table with Clay's dinner. Vanner stood up. "We've got a good cook," he said. "Enjoy your meal."

He stopped and glanced down. "And when you start blaming Mr. Damson for all your troubles, Belden, stop and ask yourself what he would want with your land. He has enough of his own. And ask yourself too — who really profits if you leave the valley?" He smiled his thin smile and walked quietly away.

X

Clay rode the dun slowly through the valley and down the road toward the warm lights of the Winged L ranch house. Vanner had been right in one thing, he had to admit. The beefsteak and potatoes the cook at the Cattlemen's had whipped up were better than anything he had tasted in quite a while.

Outside of that, he reflected sourly, he had wasted his time going to the saloon. Molly had not appeared again while he was there. And all he had got from Vanner was the uneasy knowledge that Vanner's talk meant more than Clay was able to read into it. There was a threat to someone besides himself in Vanner's soft-spoken words, but he couldn't put his finger on anything solid.

He swore in helpless frustration and pushed the dun a little faster down the moon-dappled road. The task that lay ahead of him wasn't going to be a pleasant one, but it had to be done and he wanted to finish it quickly and get some rest. By starting early tomorrow, he hoped to complete the job of rounding up the judge's cattle before nightfall.

He trotted the dun to the front of the big house and dismounted. He was halfway up the veranda steps when the door opened. Tom Roddy stood framed in the lamplight, looking out. Surprise flickered across his face.

"It ain't Bert. It's Clay," he called behind him.

He stepped back to let Clay step into the warm, richly furnished room. The judge and Tonia were having their after-dinner coffee before a crackling fire in the huge fireplace. With the exception of Tom Roddy, they were alone, although Clay knew their custom was to have all the hands in for coffee of an evening.

Clay had his news ready to blurt out, but now he couldn't find the words. "You're looking for Bert Coniff?" he asked finally.

"The men are hunting him up in the mountains now," the judge said. "Someone claims they saw him riding toward your place earlier."

Clay was watching Tonia. She sat with

her eyes downcast, her cheeks pink as though she was embarrassed by the memory of her outburst the last time they met.

The judge said, "Excuse our lack of welcome, but we're worried about Bert. We're afraid he might have been thrown from his horse. I can't imagine what else might have happened to him."

Clay said slowly, reluctantly, "Bert's all right. He's in jail." He saw their startled expressions and added, "I'm sorry to have to tell you this, Judge, but I caught Bert sniping at me today."

Tonia whispered, "Oh, no!" and stared at Clay with shock-widened eyes.

"That's impossible!" Judge Lyles cried.

Tom Roddy said nothing, but looked from Clay to the judge with a strangely thoughtful expression on his face. The judge rose abruptly. "Are you sure?" he demanded.

Clay explained as he had to the sheriff. When he finished, Judge Lyles strode back and forth across the room, shaking his head. "I can't believe it," he whispered. "I can't believe it." He stopped and looked pleadingly at Clay. "Did he have anything to say? Did he give any reason at all?"

"He claims he was up hunting deer.

That's all he'll say," Clay answered.

"Hunting deer in the middle of haying?" Roddy said. "That ain't what he said here. He told everybody he was feeling a little sick and was going in to see the doctor," he explained to Clay. "But I was in Doc Fraley's office a good part of the afternoon and I didn't see him at all. When I come out here and said so, one of the boys remembered thinking it was Bert he saw riding for the mountains. So after supper, they went looking for him."

The judge stopped his pacing. "I'll go talk to him," he said decisively. He nodded toward Clay. "I don't doubt your word, but there must be some reason for his doing this. He's been a good man for a long time."

Clay sensed the pain under the bewilderment in Judge Lyles' voice. He tried to find words to help the older man but none would come. The best thing to do right now, he decided, would be to let the judge be by himself for a while.

Clay moved awkwardly toward the door. "The sheriff said he'd be around this evening if you wanted to ride in and talk to Bert. Otherwise, he'll wait for you to come tomorrow."

The judge gave no sign he'd heard.

Tonia rose and touched his arm, leading him back to the couch. "Wait until tomorrow, Dad. It's too late to go out tonight." She left him and came toward Clay. She was wearing a wine-colored dress that highlighted her dark beauty, but at the moment Clay was aware only of the shock filling her eyes.

She said, "Tom, will you ride up with Clay and tell the men to come home?"

"I already figured on that," Roddy said gruffly. He murmured something to the judge, who was sitting staring at the floor, and then went quickly out a rear door.

Clay and Tonia went onto the veranda. She stopped at the top of the steps. "Clay, what do you think this means?"

"I think Damson's money got to Bert," he said flatly. He looked out over the moonlit yard. "I'm sorry I had to be the one to bring the news."

"Why didn't you bring him here instead of taking him to jail?" she cried. "At least you could have given us a chance to talk to him first!"

"Is that what the judge would have wanted? A chance to cover up for Bert?"

She lifted her head defiantly. "Is that what you think I meant?"

He recalled her strange actions of a few

115

days before. Then she hadn't seemed like the frank, forthright Tonia he had always known. He felt the same sensation of her withdrawing, holding something back from him now.

"I don't know what I think," he admitted. "I only know Bert tried to kill me. So I took him to the sheriff."

Tom Roddy came riding around the house on the old white plug he favored. Tonia said in a dull voice, "Of course. I see, Clay. Good night."

Roddy and Clay rode silently side by side until they reached the edge of Clay's land. Then Roddy said, "Don't get the wrong idea about Tonia, Clay. Remember, she came back from the coast just a little while ago. And a lot of things had changed in the short time she was gone. She just ain't got herself squared around yet to understanding them."

"She acts as if she's trying to protect somebody — from me," Clay said bluntly.

Roddy turned shrewd eyes on him. "There's only two people I know that Tonia would protect — lie for — her dad and you." He spat tobacco juice onto the moon-dappled trail. "And she'd do more than lie to help either one of you. But just remember, she can still shoot a nut out of

116

a squirrel's teeth at a hundred paces and never muss his whiskers. Under them fancy clothes and ladylike talk, she ain't much different from what she was."

"What are you driving at?" Clay demanded. "What's all this got to do with the way she's been acting toward me?"

"I'm trying to tell you," Roddy said. "She thinks a heap of both her dad and you. But if it came to a choice, the judge'd come first."

"Why should there be a choice?" Clay said angrily. "Does she believe I'm trying to hurt her father? He's my friend. Without his help, I wouldn't be able to get my ranch started. That's a foolish way to talk, Tom."

"It ain't what she believes you'd do," Roddy said. "It's what she's afraid you might think." He spat again. "She was afraid all along that Bert was the man behind the sniping. She's been out to the ranch a lot more than the judge lately, and she's known Coniff was acting funny — claiming to be sick so he could get out of working, and then disappearing for hours at a time. And then I let slip to her that Bert's been doing a lot of heavy courting these past months — at the Cattlemen's Bar. He's sweet on one of the dancing girls

Molly brings in for Saturday nights. A cowhand's pay don't buy many fancy gewgaws for a girl like that."

He added worriedly, "And what with the judge in the hole from buying extra stock and a lot of haying equipment ever since he started using your meadows for summer pasture, it don't look so good."

Clay stared at him. "Are you trying to tell me that Tonia believes the judge hired Bert to drive me away from my own land?"

"Nope. But she believes you'll get around to thinking just that one of these days," Roddy said. "Look at it her way, Clay. The judge has always been the biggest man in the valley since Tonia remembers. Now Bick Damson has got rich and he's sure trying hard to make folks think that makes him important. Now the judge is a nice man but he's human, and he didn't take friendly to being asked to share this little puddle of his with another big frog.

"He kind of puffed up the number of steers he put on your graze and he was right generous in the amount of his land he put to hay. Then he buys the fanciest haying machinery you ever did see. Went into debt doing it. Now you come back with a plan to trim that graze into a ranch

118

for yourself. What's the judge going to do when he's got no place for all that extra beef he's bought? Stands to reason he'll have to sell it off, probably taking a loss. And he'll be left with a lot of expensive hay he can't use."

He spat out his quid of tobacco and wiped his hand across his lips. "That's what they're saying in town," he told Clay. "Everyone figures your coming back is going to hurt the judge mighty bad. Tonia knew you'd hear the talk."

"She knows me better than to think I'd believe it," Clay said.

"She knows you wouldn't believe it without proof," Roddy said. "But I think she figured that once you found out Bert Coniff — one of the judge's top hands — was doing the sniping, then you'd start thinking the other way."

"That's crazy," Clay said. "The judge and I talked all this out when we met in Helena. I'm the one who wrote and told him to use my graze in the first place. And we both knew what my coming back could do to him. The judge was willing to take the chance that we'd figure out someway to get him out of the hole."

"Sure, that's like the judge," Roddy said. "He'll do anything for someone he believes in, no matter what it costs him. Everybody knows that down inside themselves. But they wouldn't be human if they didn't grab at the chance to pretend that maybe someone bigger than themselves is just as mean and ornery as big people are supposed to be."

He glanced at Clay. "And just saying that you trust the judge won't stop all the talk."

"I've thought of a way to keep the judge from losing anything by my coming back," Clay said. "I'm going to channel the water from my swamp to his dry south section and irrigate it. Then he'll have all the grass he needs. Tell *that* a round town. It will prove the judge has no reason to want me out of the valley."

"What does the judge think of that idea?" Roddy asked.

"I haven't had a chance to tell him yet," Clay admitted. "I didn't think of it until a few days ago." He swore suddenly. "I suppose since I haven't told the judge, people will still claim he hired Bert to run me off and protect himself from a big loss."

"Some sure will," Roddy said gloomily. "And Tonia doesn't know your plans either, remember. She don't believe anything against her father, but she's sure scared you might."

"She should know me better than that!" Clay exclaimed.

"How much does anybody really know anybody else?" Roddy retorted. "And anyway, most people don't think with their heads. Most of the time they think with their feelings. Take the folks in town. If they stopped to think with their heads, not one would trust Bick Damson or Kemp Vanner any farther'n they could spit. But they ain't thinking that way. They just think how fine and generous Damson is with his money, never stopping to figure that no one — least of all a bully like Damson — gives away money for nothing. They'd do better to think about what reason he might have for being generous. But it'll probably be too late when they get around to that."

"So that's why Roy Ponders doesn't want any trouble with Damson or Vanner," Clay said. "He thinks the people would side with them."

"That's right," Roddy said. "And all he wants is to get re-elected and live peaceable for the few years he's got left as a sheriff."

Clay thought of the quiet way Ponders had accepted the charges against Bert Coniff. He felt worry stir inside him as he thought Ponders might have turned more

121

politician than lawman. In that case, he would be apt to let Bert Coniff sneak out of the valley, just to avoid unpleasantness. It occurred to Clay that Ponders might already know that Vanner and Damson, rather than the judge, had hired Coniff.

Clay swore angrily. This was worse than he had thought. His catching the sniper hadn't solved anything as he had expected it to. It had only made the whispered rumors about the judge sound as if they had more truth to them. And that meant another victory for Vanner and Damson, because Clay knew without being told that Vanner must have started the rumors about Judge Lyles not wanting him to come back and build up his ranch. It was just the kind of situation a man like Vanner would take quick advantage of.

Roddy let out a soft shout. "Up ahead — that fire."

"That's my camp," Clay said. "The Winged L men are probably thawing out after looking for Bert Coniff."

They rode across the bench toward the fire. Five men were gathered around it, drinking coffee. Roddy hailed them and led the way into the camp.

"You can go home boys. Bert's been found."

Pete Apley, the Winged L foreman, grunted with relief. "It's about time," he said. He nodded at Clay. "We borrowed some of your firewood and coffee," he said.

"My pleasure," Clay replied. He looked at the tired, drawn men. He wondered how they would react after they found out about Bert Coniff. They wouldn't be happy after putting in a hard day haying to find they'd wasted cold, weary hours hunting for a man who was in jail.

Clay saw that Roddy wasn't about to break the news right now. The old man merely said, "Let's ride, boys, and let Clay roll in his blankets."

Apley and his men mounted their horses. "When you get squared away, drop in and we'll pay you back for this coffee we drunk," Apley said.

"I'll do that," Clay answered. He stood by the fire until they were out of sight. Then he unsaddled and rubbed down the dun. He picketed it on the bench and went to his blankets. He was tired all the way through, but the fire had burned to coals and he still lay awake, staring up at the night sky.

Roddy's explanations had helped him understand Tonia's strange behavior, but at the same time they had planted a cold seed of suspicion in his mind. It was crazy, he told himself, even to consider suspecting the judge. Everything Clay knew about him made it too foolish to even think about. But he couldn't shake Vanner's softly taunting words out of his head: *Ask yourself who really profits if you leave the valley.*

Not Damson. He had no use for Clay's mountainous land. Not when he already had his big hand squeezed down on a good piece of the valley. Not when he had a silver mine to bring him in all the money he needed.

Clay turned restlessly in his blankets. That mine of Damson's. Everytime he thought about it it seemed to him that there was something wrong with it. Or maybe he was just envious because a man like Damson had struck it rich. Whatever it was lay tantalizingly just beyond the reach of his mind. He finally fell asleep, the hours of wakefulness having accomplished nothing.

XI

Clay awoke with the first light and drove himself throughout the cool, sunlit day to round up the last of the judge's stock and pen them with the others corralled behind the brush fence that closed off the mouth of Deadman Canyon.

After eating his noon dinner, Clay noticed a weak spot in the fence. But the cattle were all grazing at the upper end of the canyon and he decided it was safe to leave repairs until he had the last animal inside. The fence only had to hold one more night anyway. Tomorrow he planned to get Tom Roddy and drive the whole herd down to Winged L graze.

Clay was ready to return to work when he heard horsemen coming up the trail to the bench. Quickly he put the dun in the protective angle of rock where he had his camp. He drew his rifle and laid it across his legs. Then he watched the spot where the trail came onto the bench and waited.

He let tension run out of him as he saw Roy Ponders come into view. Thrusting the rifle back in its boot, he rode out to meet the sheriff.

Ponders looked grave and drawn, as if he had been up a good part of the night. "I came to see those heelprints," he said. He indicated Bert Coniff's boot hanging from his saddlehorn.

Clay nodded and reined the dun around. "Follow me," he said briefly.

He led the way to the high meadow country. They rode single file along the narrow trails, not speaking but concentrating on helping their horses keep solid footing. Only after Clay had shown the sheriff the deadfall with its view of the dugout trail across the gorge, and the clear heelprint in the stand of pines, did Ponders break his silence.

He said, "You've heard the stories going around town about Judge Lyles?"

"From Tom Roddy, last night," Clay said.

The sheriff nodded. "The latest story seems to be that the judge hired Bert to kill you so he could keep on using your summer pasture."

"What does Coniff have to say?" Clay asked.

"That's his story too," Roy Ponders said heavily. "He wouldn't say a word last night after you left. But later, when I got back from having my dinner at the hotel, he started talking. He didn't come right out and admit anything, but he hinted pretty strong that the judge had paid him extra to be the sniper."

"That's crazy!" Clay exclaimed. "My guess is that Vanner or Damson got to Coniff and promised they'd get him free if he told you that."

"I had the same thought," Ponders admitted. "Only Vanner was with me in the hotel all the time I was there. And when I went looking for Damson, I found him sleeping off a bottle of whiskey in his room at the Cattlemen's."

"What about those men of Damson's — Marnie and Pike?" Clay asked.

"They were at the saloon," Ponders said. "Molly Doane told me they'd been there since shortly after you left the place."

"Has the judge seen Coniff yet?" Clay asked.

"This morning," Ponders replied. "All Bert would say to him was, 'You better get me out of here.' The judge didn't seem to know what Bert meant, and after I explained what Bert had told me last night, he just went to his house without saying a word."

A shadow of worry passed over the sheriff's face. "The judge collapsed when he got home. He's down in bed right now." He shook his head. "He isn't the strongest man in the world. Doc Fraley told me his heart is weak. Another shock like this could kill him, Doc says. Tonia and Roddy are keeping the judge quiet. They all aim to stay in town."

Clay said, "When you go back, tell the judge this. Maybe it'll help make him feel a little better." He explained his plan to divert water to the judge's dry section and so solve the problem of what to do with the extra cattle.

"He and Roddy were talking about that when I was at the house," the sheriff said. "It seemed to cheer the judge considerably." He added almost slyly, "And Tonia too."

"Maybe you and Tom can get the word around town," Clay said. "Let's see if that won't stop the rumors Vanner started."

"If Vanner started them," Ponders said.

"Who else would?" Clay demanded. "Haven't you seen and heard enough to know Judge Lyles wouldn't hire Bert to kill me!"

"The job of the law is to consider all possibilities," Roy Ponders said. "I know what a fine man the judge has always been. But people change — especially where money is concerned. And there's just enough truth to the rumors to make a man stop and think. Your building a ranch up here could have ruined the judge. He's that much in debt to the bank."

"But that's all changed," Clay pointed out. "Once his south section gets water, he won't have to worry."

"But he didn't know that until today," Ponders said. He looked closely at Clay. "You and I both know the judge well, but didn't the idea he might be behind Bert Coniff ever cross your mind?"

"It did," Clay admitted. "But not for long."

"I feel the same way, but as the law I can't throw the idea aside," the sheriff said. He turned his horse. "I'll be getting back. With the evidence I just saw, there's no doubt Bert will have to stand trial. I might as well get the proceedings going."

Clay stayed where he was. "Tell Tom I could use some help tomorrow. I'll have all the stock ready to drive down to the valley."

The sheriff nodded. Clay watched him until he disappeared and then went higher up to scour the mountain for the last few cattle.

He was tiring as he drove the final six head through gathering dusk toward the bench. He pushed there faster than he liked, fighting the chill of the quickening October night. When he reached the bench, it was that hour between dark and moonrise when everything seemed blackest and nothing had a solid shape about it. Clay could barely make out the tall spires of rock marking the mouth of Deadman Canyon.

He breathed weary relief as he made a small opening in the fence and drove the cattle through it and into the rest of the gather waiting at the upper end of the blind draw. He was about halfway up it when he heard the two sharp, quick rifle shots.

They had come from behind him, from somewhere outside the meadow. He turned in the saddle but could see nothing in the darkness. Suddenly a handgun tore apart the cool quiet of the night. Clay swung back toward the end of the canyon. A second shot blossomed fire against the darkness. A voice whooped wildly and the gun fired again.

Clay reached for his rifle. He heard the cattle stirring and realized what was happening. Who ever had fired those rifle shots had done so to warn someone waiting up at the far end of the canyon that Clay was coming. Then the man inside had used his handgun to start the cattle moving down the canyon.

In the hope, Clay thought, of catching him in a stampede of wild cattle running in panic through the dark night!

The cattle were moving about nervously, pawing at the grass, surging this way and that in a formless mass. The man with the handgun fired again. His voice rose in a shrill, frightening whoop. Clay lifted his rifle and set a flurry of shots into the darkness above the cattle. He heard the growing thunder of their hoofbeats. The ground began to tremble. A final shot roared against the night and the cattle broke into a terror-driven stampede.

Clay turned the dun and raked his heels across its flanks. The horse broke into a hard run toward the mouth of the draw, desperately seeking to keep ahead of the surging wave of crazed beeves.

Clay and the dun reached the opening in the brush fence less than a dozen feet ahead of the first cattle. Clay put the horse through the narrow opening and reined it to the left, in an attempt to angle across the bench and reach the protection of the big rock by his camp. The dun stumbled as one hoof hit soft dirt at the edge of a chuckhole. It lost its stride and nearly went down as the herd hit the brush fence.

Clay jerked the dun's head up. "Run!" he shouted over the cracking of the shattered fence.

The dun caught its stride and raced for the far side of the bench. A long-legged steer came out of nowhere and cut across the horse's path. The dun pulled up short, neighing in terror. The abrupt stop lifted Clay out of the saddle. He bit the ground with his shoulder, grunting with shock as the air was driven out of his lungs. The dun galloped for the safety of the camp.

Clay scrambled to his feet and ran after the horse. Cattle were flowing over the bench now, scattering in blind panic. A head-tossing cow struck Clay's back a glancing blow as she ran past. He stumbled and pitched forward. He hit the shoulder of rock, fell back, and staggered forward. He went to his knees at the edge of his cold campfire and then slid onto his face and lay still.

He could feel the dun's moist nose nuzzling his neck and he sat up dazedly. Clay looked around and realized he must have blacked out. The moon had come up and the bench was flooded with its cold white light.

He staggered to his feet and went to his water supply. He poured icy water over his face and neck and took a long, deep drink. He walked to the edge of his camp and looked at the silent, empty bench. The cattle had disappeared. There was only the broken fence and the torn grass to show they had ever existed.

Days of work lost, Clay thought bitterly. Maybe a lot of the judge's prime beef lost. He knew he would be lucky if he didn't find more than one animal with a broken leg or worse come daylight.

As his head cleared, anger worked into him more deeply. He recalled the two rifle shots that came just before the stampede started. It was plain enough that someone had been watching him from the hills alongside the bench, and had sent a signal to whoever waited inside as soon as Clay rode into the canyon. Then the trap had been sprung.

The stampede could have been started for only one reason — to kill him and make his death look like an accident. And

Clay knew only one man in the Wildhorse country who would have bothered with such a devious scheme — Kemp Vanner.

Clay caught the dun and climbed into the saddle. He headed the horse angrily down the trail leading to the hill road and Bick Damson's house.

XII

Damson's house lay dark and silent under the bright moon. Clay was about to ride past and on to town when a flicker of lantern light reflecting from the tops of pine trees caught his attention. He turned the dun to the left, up the rutted road that led to Damson's mine.

He slowed the horse as he started up a low rise. If Damson knew that he was still alive, this could be a trap. The lights could have been put here by the mine to make him do just what he was doing — trespassing.

Damson and Vanner would like that, Clay thought. It would put him in a position where they could shoot him with justification. He shook his head, still unable to understand why Vanner was willing to go to such lengths to drive him out of the valley or kill him.

He neared the top of the rise and reined in the dun. Quietly, he slid to the ground and walked forward, moving in the shadow of tall pines lining the side of the road. He pulled up short when he could see down into the hollow where Damson had his mine.

Damson was there, framed in the light from a trio of lanterns hanging from the barren branch of a lightning-struck tree. He was stripped to the waist and his powerfully-muscled body gleamed with sweat as he swung a shovel rhythmically, filling the big box of an ore wagon.

Damson's apparent lack of concern warned Clay to caution. The big man seemed to be completely alone, and his gun and belt lay with his shirt some distance away, out of reach. Yet he moved as confidently as though his crew were protecting him. Or as if he had nothing to worry about because Clay was dead.

Clay looked carefully around. The lanterns cast a wide swath of light, showing him the pile of ore where Damson worked, the big freight wagon he was loading, the hand-driven ore car that sat at the mouth of the mine entrance. Beyond the light, shadows lay thick and heavy and motionless. If anyone was around, he was too well hidden for Clay to find.

He turned his eyes back to the pile of ore. As it had before, a feeling of wrongness tugged at his mind. His gaze traveled from the ore to the tunnel entrance of Damson's mine. It was no more than a hole cut out of a mound of the heavy clay soil that formed this part of the foothills.

Heavy clay soil! An idea danced tantalizingly on the edge of Clay's mind. He stared at the empty ore car, with its rusted wheels sitting on narrow, rusted tracks.

And then he knew. The pile of ore Damson was shoveling hadn't come from his mine. It hadn't come from anywhere close to here. Two years of swinging a pick in silver mines had taught Clay a good deal of practical geology. And one thing he had learned — metal bearing ores didn't exist in the heavy clay Damson had here.

Clay retreated, slipping quietly from tree to tree until he reached the dun. He led it down the road until he was sure he was out of Damson's earshot. Then he mounted and headed the dun back along the wagon road to his own land.

He rode a half mile before he found a deer trail leading up into the hills. He followed it, going slowly now as the ground grew steep. He reasoned that Damson was bringing in ore from someone else's land and claiming it had come from his own mine. But Damson couldn't haul the ore openly, and that meant he had to have a back trail over which he could carry the ore to the mine.

Clay swung the dun in an arc, working into the hills and, at the same time, back in the general direction of Damson's mine. Exultation swept over him as he broke down a slope and onto a wide trail. It was of fairly recent construction and had been used a good deal lately. The prints of pack animals showed clearly in the bright moonlight. He turned away from the mine and rode in a southerly direction, back-tracking the pack road.

The trail was fairly level, following canyon bottoms where it could, crawling over hills only when there was no way around them. Finally it began to rise, twisting its way upward to break suddenly through thick timber and onto the wagon road that led over the pass and out of the valley.

Clay hurried the dun across the wagon road and looked back. There was no sign of the trail he had just left. The stand of trees hid it completely. He turned and scanned the timber lining the near side of the wagon road. If he hadn't been looking for the trail to start up again, he wouldn't have seen it at all. The beginning had been cleverly camouflaged by brush and timber so that it was almost invisible.

Clay pushed the dun through the brush and went on. He judged that the trail crossed the pass road about halfway to the summit, and now he saw that it was climbing again.

Clay came out onto a wide flat and stopped. There was no need to go farther. Not tonight. He was on his own land. From here this trail could lead to only one place — the great tumble of rocks above the rear of Deadman Canyon.

Anger shook Clay. Damson had grown rich and powerful from silver that belonged to him! Now Clay understood what a man like Vanner was doing in Wildhorse. A scheme as difficult to carry out as this one needed the kind of mind Damson didn't have. And Damson was just smart enough to figure that out. He'd deliberately brought Vanner here to help him rob Clay of silver while making it look as though the ore came from Damson's own mine.

Either that or Vanner had found the silver first and picked Damson as the man best suited to front for him. It didn't make much difference which one had the idea first. Clay figured Roy Ponders' jail was big enough to hold them both.

He pushed the dun back the way he had come. He rode past the point where he'd first found this trail. A short distance beyond he could see the lantern lights reflecting off the trees again. He was almost back to Damson's mine. But this time he was coming in from a different direction.

The trail led around a timbered hill, went over a short rise, and dropped abruptly into the hollow where Damson was working. Clay rode into the circle of lantern light and pulled the dun up short, drawing his gun.

Damson was standing with his shovel half-raised, a puzzled expression on his face as he squinted toward Clay. The shovel fell out of his hands and he took a backward step.

"Belden! I thought —"

"Your boys told you wrong," Clay interrupted. "Vanner's scheme misfired. Sorry to disappoint you, Damson."

Damson ran his tongue over his lips. His eyes moved past Clay to the trail Clay had left. The question he wanted to ask lay openly on his heavy face.

Clay said obligingly, "I found your pack trail." He glared at the pile of ore beside Damson. "That looks pretty rich from here. How much do you figure I'm worth — counting what you've already turned into money?"

"It's mine!" Damson shouted at him. "I found it. By God, you'll get nothing from me."

He made a move toward his gun. "Hold it right there!" Clay ordered sharply. Damson took a stride forward. Clay fired. His bullet hit Damson's gun and sent it flying off the darkness. Damson dropped to the ground as if he thought the bullet had hit him.

Clay said with disgust, "Get to your feet. We're riding to town."

Damson got up and walked toward Clay. He held both hands at his sides, his huge fists clenched. Suddenly he lifted his right arm and swung it. Clay saw the chunk of ore Damson held in his striking hand and knew that, the big man had pretended fear at Clay's shot, but had fallen to the ground as a blind. Clay ducked to shield himself from the chunk of ore, but he was too slow. The rock caught his gun arm at the elbow, numbing it. He felt the gun slide from his fingers.

Damson made a dive for the gun as it struck the ground. Clay left the saddle in a leaping dive that brought him down on Damson's back.

Damson straightened up, flinging Clay off. Clay hit the ground and rolled. Damson turned and gave a gusty laugh. He came at Clay with a shoulder-swinging rush. Muscles bulged under his sweat-streaked skin. He moved quickly on his thick, solid legs, his fists clenched into hard boulders of bone and flesh.

Clay felt a sudden savage pleasure. He measured himself against Damson and he knew that Damson had never stood a better chance of whipping him than now. The long hard day in the saddle and the bruising he had taken during the stampede had honed away the sharp edge of his strength. But still he relished this chance to fight Damson without interference from anyone.

He set himself as Damson's bull-like rush picked up speed and power.

Damson reached Clay and swung a heavy right first. Clay side-stepped. Too late he saw that Damson's left fist held a piece of ore as well. Damson threw the rock. Clay flung an arm up over his eyes. The ore struck the arm a glancing blow and went on to slam against his forehead, right between his eyes. For an instant he was blinded. He staggered backward.

Damson's gusty laugh came again. He stepped in and rapped a fist over Clay's heart. He swung from far down and crashed his fist to Clay's temple.

Clay went to his knees, blinking against the blinding tears scalding his eyes. He saw Damson through a haze of moisture. Damson came slowly toward him, lifting a leg to drive a boot toe into his face. Clay twisted aside as the boot gouged air beside his head. He reached up and caught Damson's ankle. He jerked, twisting backwards.

Damson fought to hold his balance, lost it, and crashed to the ground. Clay climbed to his feet and rubbed his eyes. He saw Damson rise slowly, stand for a moment shaking his head like a wounded bull, and then move slowly forward.

Clay could see more clearly now, and he let Damson come almost up to him before he moved. He side-stepped as Damson swung. This time he ducked his head and moved in, rapping his left hand against Damson's nose. He danced back and let Damson rush again. Clay blocked a right and drove two solid blows to Damson's heart. Damson gave ground, pain whitening his heavy mouth. Clay pressed him, chopping both fists into Damson's eyes.

Damson got in one more swing, a hard chop to the side of Clay's head that sent him spinning off balance. And then Clay knew it was over. His crashing fall and Clay's coldly calculated fists had broken Damson. His movements were slow; his eyes had begun to glaze.

Clay drove him across the hollow until he had Damson against the side of the freight wagon. Damson made a feeble effort to bring up his guard but Clay brushed it aside and chopped as methodically as a surgeon at Damson's unprotected face.

Damson swung wildly, blinded by blood streaming from cuts above his eyes. Clay split his lips open and blood dribbled down over his chin and onto the hair matting his chest. Relentlessly, Clay continued swinging. He felt bone and cartilage give as his fists found Damson's nose. He swung a final harsh blow against the side of Damson's head and then stepped back, waiting for Damson to fall.

Damson pawed at the air but stayed upright, his back pressed to the side of the freight wagon. Clay stepped in and hit him in the Adam's apple. Damson retched.

Clay drove a fist under Damson's breast-bone.

Damson went down to his knees. He stayed that way, his head hanging, blood dripping from his battered face. After a long moment he lifted his head and wiped a little of the blood away from his eyes so he could see Clay.

"I'll kill you for this. So help me."

"Your privilege," Clay said. "If you're still young enough when you get out of jail."

Damson cried out wildly and pushed himself forward in a diving charge that struck Clay around the legs. Clay went over backward with Damson clinging to him. He twisted free and rolled to where his gun had fallen. Damson scrambled to his feet and staggered to Clay's dun. He flung himself on its back and kicked it savagely. The horse bolted along the rutted road.

Clay got the gun and surged to his feet. He fired once, aiming high. The dun skittered sideways. Damson, barely in the saddle, lost his grip and went down in the brush along the road. He picked himself up and ran over the rise and out of sight.

Clay reached the top of the rise in time to see Damson out of gun range now, stagger across the hill road and down toward his house. Clay heard the tired dun hammering its way toward town. Swearing, he started wearily after it.

XIII

Damson staggered into his house and found a rifle. He went out on the veranda and searched the moonlit yard for signs of Clay. He saw nothing and he stumbled across the yard and plunged his face into the horse trough.

He came up blowing, cursing at the sting of the water on his cuts. He pumped fresh water and let it stream over his head. His eyes cleared and he went back into the house. He put on a shirt and buckled on a gun and belt. Then he hurried to the barn and saddled his palomino. He kicked it savagely down to the valley road and toward town.

He swung to the west so that he would come up to the Cattlemen's Bar by way of Ted Petrie's livery stable and not have to pass the jail. He reached the saloon by the back alley and put the horse in the small stable there. He ran into the building through the rear door and climbed the stairs to the hallway.

He went down the hall to Vanner's room and tried the door. It was locked. He rapped on it and heard only a hollow echo. Swearing, he retreated to Molly's door. He flung it open. She was at her desk as she had been the last time he came in here. She looked up questioningly.

Surprise widened her eyes. "What happened to you?"

"Never mind. Get Vanner up here and be quick about it. And don't give me none of your lip this time!" he shouted.

Molly made no move to get up and he cried, "I said, be quick!" He turned and hurried to his own room where he could get a drink.

He was a little calmer when Vanner came into the room. Vanner shut the door. "What is it this time? I told you —" He stopped and stared at Damson's battered face. "What kicked you?"

"Belden!" Damson said. "Marnie tells me Belden's dead. So I go on doing just what you said for me to do — shoveling ore, making myself handy for anyone who wants to find out where I am."

He broke off and took another drink.

148

"And who comes riding up our trail but Belden!" He glared at Vanner. "He found out about the mine. He knows what we been up to. He tried to take me to jail, by God!"

Vanner pursed his lips thoughtfully. "And you had a fight," he murmured. Then he looked at Damson sharply. "What did you do with his body, leave it lying where the sheriff can find it?"

Damson cursed him viciously. "There ain't no body," he shouted. "He beat me, whipped me into the dirt. I was lucky to get away."

Vanner paled. "You let Belden loose — to come into town and tell the law what he found out?"

"I stole his horse and then lost it," Damson said. "I figure I got here first. Leastways I didn't see a whisker of Belden on my way into town." He took a deep breath. "What are you going to do now?"

Vanner clenched his fists and then slowly relaxed them. His lips moved but no sound came out. Finally he said, "I'll have to hurry our plans." His voice was bitter. "That fool Marnie told me Belden was dead, too."

"Wait'll I get my hands on him!" Damson began.

"He's gone," Vanner said shortly. "I fixed it with Molly so she'll swear he and Pike have been locked in a room here ever since late afternoon. The story is they came in and got drunk and she put them away to sleep it off. That was to protect them if there was any question about Belden's death. And to keep them from being accused of shooting Bert Coniff. That's where Marnie's gone now. He's waiting to shoot Coniff."

"Once Belden sees the sheriff, Ponders will know who did it, all right!" Damson cried.

"It's too late now," Vanner said. He looked at his pocket watch. "In just three minutes, two drifters are going to start a fight down by Petrie's livery stable. That will draw the sheriff out of the jail. Then Marnie'll shoot Coniff and come back here." He shrugged and smiled thinly. "And what can the sheriff prove? Molly'll stick to the story I gave her to tell."

"To hell with Marnie!" Damson shouted. "Let him hang. It's Belden I want taken care of."

Vanner turned toward the door. "I'll handle that right now," he said. "I have a dozen men downstairs mixing with the town men, buying them drinks, letting them win poker hands. The locals are all pretty drunk now. It won't take much to fire them up when they hear Coniff's been shot."

He nodded. "We'll have to do more than we planned," he murmured. "Just throwing suspicion on Judge Lyles and threatening to lynch Roddy won't be enough — not with Belden still alive."

"Stop talking and do something!" Damson yelled.

"I am doing something," Vanner said. "I'm thinking." He nodded again. "My plan was to take over the town gradually as people gained confidence in us and lost confidence in Judge Lyles. But we haven't time for that." He struck his fist into his palm. "We'll take over tonight!"

Damson stared at him. "Take over what?"

"The town," Vanner said contemptuously. "I'll make a real lynch mob out of those fools downstairs. Drunk as they are, and with my men pushing them, they'll do our work for us."

He smiled his cold, thin smile at Damson. "By morning," he said softly, "this town will need a new judge and a new sheriff."

"What about Belden?" Damson demanded.

"Stop harping on Belden," Vanner said. "What can he do to us? By tomorrow, there won't be any sheriff for him to complain to. And if you don't want to wait for tomorrow, go kill him yourself when he comes into town. Go do it now!"

"By God," Damson said, "I will!"

He took another drink and strode to the door. He paused, frowning. Then he jerked the door open suddenly and looked into the hall.

"I thought I heard someone out there."

"You've had too much whiskey as usual," Vanner said. "The bartender has orders to let no one up here without permission."

"What about that woman of yours?" Damson demanded.

"Molly? What would she be listening at doors for?" Vanner asked.

"I don't trust her," Damson grunted.

"Because she doesn't like you?" Vanner's voice was thinly contemptuous. "Can you blame her, after the way you mauled her around? I understand Belden beat you worse when he caught you at it than he did tonight."

Damson took an angry stride forward, his arm raised. He let it drop and walked back to the sideboard for another drink.

Vanner glanced at his watch again.

"Don't get impatient," he said. He went to a window and pulled the curtain aside carefully. From the window he had an angle view to the street running in front of the jailhouse. He glanced from his watch to the building and back.

"Just about now," he said softly.

Damson joined him as the sound of gunshots rose over the babble of voices and music coming from the saloon below. "What's that?"

"That's the fight the sheriff is going to attend to in a minute," Vanner said with satisfaction. "Look there!"

A man appeared from the direction of the lower part of town. He ran across the street and into the jailhouse. He reappeared with Roy Ponders. They moved quickly across the street and out of sight.

"By God," Damson said. "I —"

"Be quiet and listen!" Vanner commanded.

A gun barked sharply from somewhere behind the jail. A horse neighed shrilly and its hoofbeats hammered the night air as it ran south at full gallop.

"There!" Vanner said with satisfaction. "Give Marnie a few minutes to get back here. Then you can go hunt for Belden."

"Back here?" Damson echoed. "It

sounded to me like he was heading the other way."

Vanner chuckled. "That was Tom Roddy's old white horse you heard. One of my men stole it earlier. Marnie turned it loose after he took care of Bert Coniff. If there are any doubts, we'll be able to find plenty of witnesses who can say they saw Roddy's horse running down the back alley for its home stall. Roddy can claim he wasn't in the saddle, but by the time he thinks of a way to prove that, it will be too late." He nodded at Damson. "Far too late for him."

A short, sharp sound as of someone sliding up a window made Damson turn. "Marnie," Vanner said. "Now I have work to do." He started for the door.

"By God, you better do it good for a change," Damson said warningly. "Or it's the last chance we get."

"You take care of Belden and let me worry about the rest of it," Vanner said as he walked out.

XIV

Clay found the dun grazing by the side of the road a good two-thirds of the way to town. He climbed wearily into the saddle and urged the horse forward. He had lost too much time. Damson would have got to town and warned Vanner some time ago.

Weary as Clay was, he rode alertly, his rifle across his knees, peering ahead at every shadow along this last mile to town. He more than half-expected an ambush from Damson or his men, and he was surprised when he reached the turn-off to the judge's house without having seen anyone.

He rode downslope into the judge's rear yard. His first impulse had been to go on to the jail and report to Roy Ponders, but when he saw light spilling from the big house, he decided to stop there first. This time he wanted no misunderstandings. He would tell the judge first what happened before taking his story to the sheriff.

He reined the dun in near the back veranda and climbed the steps to the kitchen door. His knock brought quick footsteps. Tonia flung open the door.

She stared at him, her eyes widening with concern. "Clay, what happened? You look . . ." She broke off and tugged him inside. "But thank heaven you're here. There's something strange going on in town."

Clay followed her into the parlor. The judge was sitting in a wheel chair by the fireplace. His face was white and drawn from his illness, but, when he looked up, Clay saw that his eyes had the same vital force as always.

"You look like you've been fighting wildcats," he observed dryly.

"Bick Damson," Clay said briefly.

He found a chair and sat down. Dropping his hat to the floor, he began to shape a cigarette. "I found out tonight why Damson and Vanner drove people off my land," he said.

"You're convinced that Damson and Vanner were behind Bert Coniff?" the judge asked in a strange voice.

Clay lifted his eyes from the cigarette paper and met the judge's gaze squarely.

"If you mean, did I believe the stories going around that you wanted me out of the way — the answer is no."

He looked toward Tonia. "I thought before it was Damson. And now I'm sure of it."

Tonia flushed as she realized the words were meant for her. She said in a low voice, "How did you find out — beat the truth out of Damson?"

"Tonia!" her father said sharply. He shook his head at Clay. "One minute she's mad at you for challenging Damson; the next she talks about how you can whip him." He waved a hand, brushing the matter aside, and studied Clay with troubled eyes.

"Just what did you find out?"

Clay told them briefly about the stampede and how he had found the trail from Damson's mine to his own land. He said, "I tried to bring Damson in to jail, but he got away on my horse and had a good start before he lost it. He must have been a good half-hour ahead of me getting to town. Vanner's been warned."

The judge glanced up at Tonia. "I wonder if those shots we heard awhile ago have any connection with this?"

"What shots?" Clay demanded.

"A while ago — maybe twenty minutes or so — we heard some shots," the judge explained. "I sent Tom to investigate. What worries me is he hasn't come back, but his old white horse came running into the yard still saddled and bridled. Tonia and I were just wondering what we'd better do about it when you came."

"Horse might have thrown him," Clay said. He got to his feet.

Tonia said, "But Tom didn't take his horse. He walked. He rubbed the horse down this afternoon and put it in the stable. That's what we can't understand — how it got out with his saddle on it."

The judge worried the edge of the robe covering his legs. "If Doc Fraley didn't have me rooted in this contraption, I'd go see for myself. I —" He stopped abruptly as the rear door was flung open and someone ran toward the parlor.

It was Tom Roddy. He came in, red-faced and panting. He held his ancient long-barreled rifle in his hand. He ran to a desk and rummaged through a drawer.

"Tom, where have you been? What's happened?" Tonia demanded.

He got a box of cartridges from the drawer and pushed them into his pocket. "All hell's busted loose in town," he gasped. "Someone shot Bert Coniff right in his cell and they're saying it was me did it."

He seemed to see Clay for the first time. "Me and you," he corrected. "Ted Petrie and a bunch of those other fools that hang around the Cattlemen's is drunk and ornery. And all those strangers that drifted in here the last few days is egging 'em on to get the sheriff to arrest us."

"Where is the sheriff?" Clay demanded. "Where was he when Coniff was shot?"

"Some drifters started a fight down by Petrie's livery stable," Roddy answered. "Roy went down to stop it, and while he was gone someone rode up to the cell window and shot Bert dead. I seen it," he added.

"Who was it?" the judge demanded.

Roddy shook his head. "I was at the end of the alley, too far away to recognize anybody. But he came riding up on a horse that looked just like my old white. He takes one shot through the window and then jumps to the ground. He slapped the horse off in one direction and started running away in the other."

"It *was* your horse, Tom," Tonia said worriedly. "It came home a little while ago, saddled and bridled."

"Vanner!" Clay exclaimed. "That's just the kind of scheme he'd think up. He had Tom's horse stolen so people would see it right after the shooting and think Tom was the one who killed Bert."

Roddy hoisted his old rifle. "It don't much matter who thought up the idea," he said. "It's got out of hand now. I tried to follow the killer. I ain't so spry any more and he outran me. But he was heading for the Cattlemen's and I snuck up to the back door. What I heard sounded more like a meeting than respectable drinking. That's when I found out those strangers are stirring up the town to get you and me arrested."

"Where do you think you're going with that rifle?" the judge asked.

"I figure to give Roy Ponders a hand," Roddy said. "I saw him after I left the Cattlemen's. He's pretty wound up and he ain't about to let no mob tell him who to arrest."

Clay said flatly, "You stay here, Tom." He jerked his head in the direction of the judge sitting helplessly in his wheel chair. He started for the back door.

"Where are you going?" Tonia cried.

"I'm going to get the man who shot Bert Coniff and take him to the sheriff," Clay said. "I've seen drunken mobs in action

160

before. There's a chance of stopping them if we can show them the real killer."

He strode on out and jumped into the saddle. He rode to the alley that paralleled the main street, running behind the judge's property and the jail. He pushed the dun along until he was within a block of the center of town. Then he rode in a wide loop that brought him to the back of the Cattlemen's along much the same route Bick Damson had taken earlier.

Clay left the dun in the alley and went in through the back door. He moved quietly down the small hallway, past the stairs and the storeroom, to the door that opened onto the saloon.

He could hear no sounds at all — no voices, no music, no stomping of dancers. Frowning, he pulled the door open a crack and peered into the big room. It was deserted. No bartender stood behind the empty bar. No dealers shuffled cards at the tables. The four girls who were hired to dance with the men on Saturday nights weren't waiting in chairs against the wall. The room was empty.

Clay shut the door carefully and hurried softly to the rear stairs. He went up them quietly and padded down the hall to a small window that looked down on the street. A low muttering rose, swelling like a rising wind running through a pine forest. Clay pulled the curtain aside and peered out.

The town square was filled with restlessly surging men. Clay recognized many of them — small ranchers, cowhands, local businessmen, the ones who always brought their trade to the Cattlemen's Bar. The rest were strangers, hard-faced, sullenlipped men moving purposefully through the crowd, stopping to whisper something to a local man and then moving on to another.

Clay searched the crowd for Damson or Vanner. But there was no sign of either man, or of Marnie and Pike.

A low cry came from one of the rooms opening onto the hall. Clay turned. The cry grew louder and he recognized Molly's voice. He walked quickly back toward the stairs. A crash came from the end room and then the sound of a hand brutally striking flesh.

Clay jerked at the latch on the door. It refused to give and he drew back his leg and rammed his boot heel into the wood beneath the lock. The door frame splintered and Clay stumbled forward. He had a glimpse of Molly Doane sprawled on the floor, one hand to her cheek. Pike was behind Molly's desk, his feet on the top, scarring the gleaming wood. He held a gun in one big hand. Marnie stood over Molly, his arm raised.

Pike's feet came down with a crash as Clay came into the room. Marnie turned, one hand reaching for his gun. Pike surged out of the chair, bringing his gun to bear on Clay. Clay's arm moved in a swift draw. He dropped to his knees and cleared leather just as Pike fired. The bullet ripped out a piece of the door casing.

Clay fired his .44 twice. A hole appeared where Pike's nose had been and he went over the desk chair and fell heavily to the floor. Molly cried, "Clay, watch out!"

He turned to see Marnie drawing a fine bead on him. The little man's lips were pulled back over his teeth in an eager grimace. He fired just as Molly Doane reached out and jerked at his leg.

Marnie's shot plowed into the floor as he lost his balance. He caught himself like a cat and fired again before Clay could swing around in his direction. The bullet raked Clay along the thigh, driving him off his feet.

Molly was clawing at Marnie's leg, trying to pull him down. Clay rolled to his knees in time to see Marnie lift his gun in order to bring the barrel down on Molly's head. Clay snapped a single quick shot. It caught Marnie in the side of the throat. He stood upright for a moment with the grimace still pulling at his lips. Then he fell, his gun arm doubling under him.

Clay got up and hurried to Molly. She looked at the bullet burn on his thigh. "Just a scratch," she said in relief. She pushed him toward the door. "Get out of here," she cried, "before someone comes up and finds you!"

Clay said, "There isn't anybody downstairs. They're all out in the street."

She stared down at Marnie and then turned, burying her face in Clay's chest. A shudder ran through her.

"What's been going on in here?" Clay demanded. "What were those two doing in your room?"

She said swiftly, "I overheard Kemp and Bick Damson planning to turn the mob loose on you and Tom Roddy. I tried to make Kemp stop, but he wouldn't listen."

She stepped back and lifted her head, looking searchingly into Clay's face. "Kemp knows how I've always felt about you, Clay and he hates you because of that. When you first came back here, he told me

I could take my choice. I could leave him or I could stay — and help him. But I couldn't have him and go on wanting you too!"

Her voice dropped. "I made my choice. Kemp gave me things. The things I never had before and never hoped to get. I — I thought I wanted that more than anything. But when I heard him planning to get rid of you and Tom Roddy and then take over the town, I knew I couldn't just stand by and let it happen."

"Where is Vanner now?" Clay asked.

"Out where he can make things happen without being involved himself," she said bitterly. "When he wouldn't listen to me, I tried to run — to get to Roy Ponders and warn him. Kemp caught me and turned me over to Marnie and Pike for safekeeping. Marnie put his hands on me. I fought him and he knocked me down."

Clay said gently, "It's all over now. All you have to do is tell the mob the truth and they'll forget about making the sheriff arrest Tom and me. Once they hear how Damson's been stealing silver from my land, they'll go looking for him, not us."

"You don't understand," she cried. "Those men Kemp brought into town filled Ted Petrie and the other local men

165

full of whiskey and talk. They aren't just getting them to have you and Tom arrested. They want you lynched! And they know the sheriff and the judge will try to protect you — and be destroyed. That's Kemp's idea — to let the mob get rid of everyone who stands in his way. By tomorrow, he plans to control the valley!"

A swelling roar from the mob outside turned Clay. He could hear his name and Tom Roddy's being shouted. He limped into the hall and down to the window at the end. Molly followed quickly.

Clay drew aside the curtain and looked out. The mob had shifted its position. It flowed in a great shapeless mass down the street, the men in front almost opposite the jailhouse door. Roy Ponders stood there, his legs planted firmly, a shotgun in his gnarled fists.

"Stay back!" he cried. "I told you men I'd do my arresting after I make an investigation. Now get back to your drinking and let me go about my business."

Ted Petrie stood swaying in the front rank of the mob. He waved a big fist in the air. "You know as well as we do that Roddy or Belden shot Bert Coniff in the back, Sheriff! What are you waiting for — advice from their friend the judge?"

A man at the rear of the crowd shouted, "I say let's get Roddy and Belden ourselves, If the sheriff won't jail 'em, we will."

"Jail, hell!" another man bellowed. "Let's take care of the dirty murderers right now!"

"That's right," the first man called loudly. "We know where Roddy is. Let's hang him!"

The crowd began to chant Roddy's name. Men in the rear pressed forward, pushing the local men in the front ranks down the dusty street.

Ponders raised his gun higher. "Stand back!" he cried. "I'll shoot the first man who goes south of this doorway."

A gun barked above the shouts of the mob. Ponders staggered and spun sideways, hitting the doorframe with his shoulder. The shotgun fell from his hands. He dropped to his knees, groping blindly for it.

The local men stopped, staring, momentarily hushed. But pressure from behind forced them slowly forward. Voices began to cry out again, calling Roddy's name in an effort to whip the drunken men back to their former frenzy.

Clay said swiftly, "Give me a minute to get out of here. Then open the window and try to make that mob listen to you. Tell them I'm in here. Then when it's safe, get away. Come to the Winged L."

Molly caught his arm. "Clay, no! They'll catch you. They'll kill you!"

"It's the only chance we have of keeping that mob away from the judge's place until we can all get out to his ranch," Clay told her. "In another minute they'll run for his house. Now do as I say."

He turned and limped down the hall. Molly cried, "Clay, be careful. Bick Damson is outside somewhere waiting to kill you."

Clay hurried on. He was at the foot of the stairs when he heard Molly's voice crying out above him. "Clay Belden is here! Hurry, before he gets away!"

Clay ran out the back door and leaped onto the dun.

XV

Clay rode the dun in a wide swing that avoided the center of town and brought him into the narrow lane running behind the jail-house. For a moment he lost track of the mob but now he could hear it surging back up the street to the Cattlemen's Bar.

The voices became muted, and Clay knew the crowd had reached the saloon. But they wouldn't stay there long, he thought. Once they found Marnie and Pike dead and him gone, they would head for the judge's house with renewed fury.

Clay slowed the dun as he neared the patches of yellow light spilling from cell windows. He remembered Molly's last warning and he searched the shadows beyond the light, seeking some sign of Damson or Kemp Vanner. He kept his .44 in his hand.

But the night was still. Clay reined the

dun in at the rear door of the jail and left the saddle. He hurried into the sheriff's office. He saw the blanket-covered mound in Bert Coniff's cell but went on without pausing.

Roy Ponders was on his knees in the doorway, his shotgun held firmly to his shoulder. He swept the empty street with deliberate eyes, as if he hoped to find some movement to shoot at.

Clay said, "Roy, get out of here quick. That mob will be starting for the judge's place any time now."

Ponders turned around and stared at Clay with glazed eyes. Blood ran down the side of his face from a bullet burn along his temple. Clay reached out to help him to his feet, but he pushed himself up, knocking aside Clay's hand. He turned away and staggered through the door.

"They went back to the Cattlemen's," he said. His voice was thick. "I knew I could stop them!"

"You stopped nothing!" Clay told him. "They went there to find me. When they see I'm gone, they'll run for the judge's place to get Tom Roddy. Now get out of here before they go crazy enough to kill you."

A sudden roar from the Cattlemen's beat

against the air. The doors crashed open and men streamed into the street. Roy Ponders took another step forward. "I'm the law!" he cried. "And they'll do as I say."

Clay grabbed at Ponders' arm, but the sheriff had started to stagger across the sidewalk. Clay swore and limped after him. "Roy, get back in here!"

He heard someone shout, "There's Belden now! By the jailhouse!"

Clay caught the sheriff at the edge of the board sidewalk. He said, "Sorry, Roy," and hit Ponders on the jaw. Ponders gazed at him in stupefied surprise and then his knees buckled. Clay caught him under the armpits and dragged him back into the jail.

A gun went off and then another. Wood splintered from the jailhouse doorframe. Clay dropped Ponders and slammed shut the door, throwing the heavy locking bar across it. The hard, sharp bark of a rifle sounded and the glass in the barred front window went in with a crash. Clay bent down and jerked the sheriff to his feet. He lifted the stocky body onto his shoulder and ran for the rear door.

He could hear men running toward the alley as he flung Ponders belly-down in front of his saddle. He climbed onto the dun and kicked it into a swift jog. A voice shouted his name as he rode through the patches of light coming from the cell windows. A gun began hammering, forcing the dun to a panicky gallop that drew it swiftly out of range.

Clay rode into the judge's rear yard and pulled up the dun by the small stable near Tom Roddy's dark and silent cottage. He slid Ponders to the ground and then slapped the dun on the flank, sending it into the safety of the stable. He bent down, intending to pick up the sheriff's limp body, when he saw a shadow move by the corner of Roddy's cottage. He straightened up and swung around, his hand reaching for his gun.

Bick Damson's heavy voice stopped him when his fingers were only inches from his gun butt. "You move again, Belden, and I'll put a bullet in your friend there. And in you too."

Damson stepped forward, into the bright moonlight. He motioned at Clay with the barrel of his gun. "Pull your gun out real easy and throw it away," he ordered. He watched Clay narrowly. "And no tricks. I know Roy ain't hurt too bad. I already had a look at him. So if you want him to stay alive a while longer, do as I say."

Clay could sense tension threading through Damson's voice. Damson wasn't used to this kind of violence, Clay decided. He was a man who had always done his fighting with his fists. He didn't seem to feel easy with a gun in his hand.

Slowly Clay drew his .44, holding the butt with the tips of his fingers. He tossed the gun toward Damson and let his arm fall back. He glanced toward the lighted house, thinking that Tom Roddy might have heard Damson and come out to investigate. But the yard was a big one, and there was no sign of anyone moving about in it.

Clay looked at Damson. "If you're going to shoot me, get it over with," he said quietly.

Damson laughed. "Why should I kill you when I can get your old friends to do it for me? Listen!"

The sound of the mob coming down the street was clear now, a ragged thudding of running feet, the crying out of drunken, angry voices.

Damson's voice thickened. "I'll tell you what's going to happen to you, Belden. You and me, we're going into that stable where it's nice and quiet. I'm going to pay you back them beatings you gave me. Then

I'll let you listen to Ted Petrie and all them other fine citizens take care of your friends in the house. After that, they can have you."

Despite the bluster in Damson's voice, Clay thought he detected something like fear beneath it. Vanner had swept him into a current a little too strong for him to swim against. And now he was giving under the strain. Why else would he risk his chance of success by taking time out to revenge himself on Clay for two bad beatings?

But, Clay realized, Damson had the time to spare, while he didn't. Every minute the crowd was drawing closer. Unless Clay could warn those inside the judge's house that the crowd wasn't demanding Tom Roddy's arrest but had come to attack and destroy, they would be unprepared. Judge Lyles was like Roy Ponders in that he assumed every man had respect enough for the law to listen to it.

Clay took a step toward the stable, at the same time moving closer to the sheriff's limp body. "If you want a fight, let's get at it," he said.

Damson brought his free hand up from his side. A rope was held in it. "You just drop down on your knees, Belden, so I can

174

throw a loop over you. Then we'll be ready to fight." His laugh had a high shrillness in it. "And don't get no ideas. I can throw a one-handed loop better'n any man in the valley."

Clay turned and watched Damson switch his gun to his left hand while he built a loop with his right. Moonlight slanted down on Damson's face, revealing the madness which had driven him to revenge himself on Clay in a bare-hand beating.

"On your knees!"

Clay took another step forward and went to his knees beside the sheriff. He leaned forward, dropping his arms down in a strangely submissive attitude. He heard the whine of the loop as Damson whirled the rope around, ready to drop it over him and pin his arms to his sides. He inched his fingers forward over the dew-damp grass. They touched the cold butt of Roy Ponders' gun.

The rope swished toward Clay. He drew the sheriff's .44 and threw himself to one side, rolling in an effort to come around facing Damson. He heard a wild curse of anger and then Damson fired. His bullet thudded into the grass where Clay had been kneeling. Clay brought the sheriff's gun up across his chest and fired while he was still moving

Damson went backwards, striking the wall of Roddy's cottage with his heavy shoulders. He lifted his gun slowly, bringing it to bear on Clay with a steady sweep. Clay stopped rolling and fired twice. Damson's body jerked. His arm dropped toward the ground and he staggered, trying to thrust himself toward Clay. His finger pulled convulsively at the trigger of his gun, emptying its bullets into the ground. He made a final effort to lift the gun, and then he collapsed, falling with his arms bent under him.

Clay got to his feet and picked up his own gun. He heard the voices of the mob coming from less than half a block up the street. He turned quickly to Roy Ponders.

The rear door of the house had been flung open and light streamed across the veranda and into the yard. "What's going on there!" Tom Roddy called.

Clay hurried into the light carrying the sheriff. "Tom," he called, "get the judge and Tonia and come on. That's a lynch mob coming!"

Tonia appeared in the doorway. "Clay?" she asked worriedly.

Clay said, "Get your father while I hitch up the team!"

A sudden burst of gunfire rattled in the air. It was followed by the sound of breaking glass and a cry of rage from Tom Roddy.

"It's too late!" he shouted. "Tonia, go get them guns out of the rack!"

Clay swore in bitter anger. He managed to run unevenly to the house, carrying the sheriff.

XVI

Clay stood at the small window set in the front door and watched the mob outside. They had been quiet since the first flurry of shots, and now some of the local men in the front rank were shifting their weight awkwardly, as if they were beginning to wish they hadn't come this far. Attacking Clay Belden or Tom Roddy was one thing, their movements seemed to say; attacking a man like Judge Lyles was something else. But Vanner's men were at work, building up drunken anger again.

Clay looked around the room behind him. Judge Lyles, his lips white-rimmed with helpless anger, was staring across the room at the shattered front window. Tom Roddy stood out of sight at the corner of the other window, his jaws working steadily on a quid of tobacco. Tonia was finishing the bandage around Roy Ponders' head.

The lamps were out but moonlight came through the broken window to light much of the room.

Clay had told them what had happened. Now the sheriff said, "Let me be, Tonia. I want to go out and talk to those fools."

"It's too late for talk," Clay said flatly. "Even if Tom and I gave ourselves up, Vanner would find a reason to get rid of the rest of you. He worked that mob up for only one reason — to take over the town and the valley with it."

Outside, someone shouted Bick Damson's name in an angry voice.

"They've found Damson's body," Clay said. "One of us had better watch the back of the house."

Tom Roddy turned from the front window and padded silently out of the room. Roy Ponders hesitated, and then picked up a carbine. He took Roddy's place.

Clay turned back to watch the street. Two of the strangers were coming into the street, carrying Damson's body with them. A murmur of anger arose. Ted Petrie staggered forward, shaking a fist in the air. "We know you're in there, Belden! Come on out. You too, Roddy! Turn 'em loose, Judge, and you won't get hurt."

Voices in the rear of the crowd shouted,

"Send them murderers out before we come and get them!"

Judge Lyles wheeled his chair forward to the broken window. Tonia ran toward him, a carbine in her hand. Clay caught her and pulled her back. "Stand by the corner of the window," he directed. "If you see anyone lift a gun, shoot!" He took a position at the outside corner where he could watch without being seen.

The judge stopped his chair in full view of those outside. "Stay where you are!" he ordered. "No man comes in here without my say so. And no man takes the law into his own hands in this valley." His voice sharpened. "Petrie, who appointed you as the law?"

Petrie hesitated and then took a bold step forward. "You're hiding killers, Judge. Who are you to talk about the law?"

The judge's voice was strong and decisive. "What court judged Belden and Roddy killers?" he demanded.

"We heard plenty of stories!" someone behind Petrie called.

"So have I," the judge called back. "I heard one tonight — one you can prove. Bick Damson and Kemp Vanner have no silver of their own. They've been stealing ore from Belden's land."

"That's Belden's story!" a voice mocked.

"Take an hour and go see for yourself," the judge challenged. "If you've appointed yourself the law, act like the law! Find the proof of a man's guilt and bring him to trial."

He leaned forward. "You, Petrie, and your friends. Would you rather be tried by a court or by a mob? Ask yourselves that!"

Voices in the rear hooted derisively, but Petrie stood with his arms at his sides. He turned and looked at the other local men behind him. "Maybe . . ." he began doubtfully.

Clay caught sudden movement at the back of the crowd. Moonlight picked out a glittering pattern of light on a quickly lifted rifle barrel. Clay raised his carbine and fired. The other gun went off, its bullet thudding above the window where the judge sat. The rifleman cried out and staggered to one side.

"Don't listen to the old fool!" someone shouted. "Get Belden and Roddy!"

Clay reached out and pulled the judge's chair behind him as other guns opened fire. Bullets scoured through the broken window and struck the back wall of the room. Tonia sighted carefully and fired twice. The shooting stopped abruptly.

Ted Petrie had a sick look on his face. "I'm leaving," he said. He tried to push his way through the crowd, other men with him followed suit. For a moment the mob was a swirling, shapeless mass. Then Petrie was thrown clear. He staggered, blinded by blood flowing from a cut on his forehead. He fell to the ground and rolled to the base of the veranda. He lay there, not trying to get up.

Angry shouts rose from the local men now. Some of them broke off from the edge of the crowd and ran awkwardly up the street. A cold, thin voice lifted out of the shadow cast by a barn across the way.

"Drive them out!" Kemp Vanner cried. "Or the judge will have you all hanging from the end of a rope. Get to cover and drive them out!"

A dozen local men were fleeing, but others stayed with Vanner's men, spreading out, finding cover behind fence posts and in shadow.

Clay searched the darkness, trying to pinpoint Vanner's position by his voice. Then he heard the swift beat of a horse galloping and he lowered his carbine. Vanner had given his orders and run for safety.

Ted Petrie rolled to his feet and made a sudden sprint up the veranda steps for the front door. A .44 rolled out its deep sound, and Petrie flung up his arms and pitched against a pillar. He fell to the porch floor and lay jerking, his hand clawing at the wood in an effort to pull himself forward.

Roy Ponders swore. "What's the matter with that crazy fool?"

"He likes our side better now," Clay said dryly. He handed the judge his carbine. "Can you cover me from this corner, sir? I'm going out and bring him in."

The judge wheeled his chair into position without bothering to reply. Clay jerked open the front door and stepped back, away from it. A hail of bullets struck the front of the house and searched through the open door. At the rear of the room a lamp shattered and the sharp smell of coal oil filled the air.

Ponders smashed the window in front of him with his gun butt and began shooting. Tonia and the judge kept up a steady cross-angled sniping. The firing from outside stopped. Clay darted out of the door and grabbed Petrie's wrists. He shambled backwards, pulling the man after him into the house.

A bullet drove wood from the edge of the

doorway as Clay went through. The judge's gun cracked sharply and a man at the edge of the yard rose up and flopped into the street. Clay rolled Petrie inside and kicked the heavy front door shut.

"Shoulder wound, I think," Clay panted. "If we can get him to Doc Fraley soon enough, he'll probably be all right."

A deep-throated burst of firing from the back of the house swung Clay around. That was Tom Roddy's gun, and it meant only one thing. There was an attack at the rear too.

Clay drew his .44 and raced into the kitchen. Tom Roddy stood by an open window, squinting along the barrel of his ancient rifle. Light flared suddenly by the stable as someone lit a torch. Roddy fired and the man carrying the torch came into sight. He stumbled across the yard and fell, crushing the flaming torch under his body.

"That's two!" Roddy said.

"And two dozen left," Clay answered. "If they ever get up courage enough to make a rush, we won't be able to stop them."

"Where are all the good citizens in this town?" Roddy demanded. "Hiding under their beds?"

"There hasn't been any trouble here for so long, few of them know what to do,"

Clay said. He started for the back door.

Roddy's gun cracked again. An answering shot struck the wall beside the window. "Where you going?" he demanded. "There's half a dozen of 'em hiding out there."

"After Kemp Vanner," Clay said. "That's the only way to stop this. With him out of the way, his men will break and run, and the others will stop when they haven't any support."

Tonia came into the kitchen. "Clay! Someone just managed to get through from town. The citizens there are gathering. If we can hold out a little while . . ."

"There's your answer," Clay said to Roddy. "They decided to crawl out from under their beds." He put his hand on the door latch. "That means the ones outside will have to hit us soon."

A torch flared at the corner of Roddy's small cottage. A voice cried, "Burn them out! Burn them out!"

Clay threw open the door and fired in the direction of the light. The man carrying the torch moved, running toward the alley. Clay said briefly, "Cover me," and stepped outside.

He slid under the porch railing to the ground and ran in a zigzag to the stable.

Behind him, Tonia and Roddy fired, sweeping every shadow. A gun blossomed flame to Clay's left. He swung in that direction and shot. The other gun went off again, aimed straight upward, and then was silent.

A bullet nicked Clay's boot heel as he threw himself into the darkness of the stable. He heard the judge's horses stirring restlessly. He made a soft clicking sound with his tongue and the dun moved cautiously forward, sniffing in his direction.

Clay caught the reins and swung into the saddle. He flattened himself over the dun's neck. Then he kicked his heels into its flanks, sending it hammering through the wide doorway and into the yard. He reined toward the alley. A gun by Roddy's cottage whipped a bullet through the dun's mane; then the crack of Tonia's carbine sounded, and the gun was still.

Clay saw torches beginning to flicker along the streets that sided and fronted the house. He kicked at the dun again, whipping it to a wild gallop toward town. He reasoned that Vanner would be directing his operation from only one place — the Cattlemen's Bar.

Once past the jailhouse, Clay made the same wide swing as before to reach the rear of the Cattlemen's Bar. He stopped and drew his gun after he'd dismounted. He climbed the steps to the upper hallway. He stopped in front of Molly Doane's door and reached for the latch.

The door opened and light flooded out, making him blink. Molly stood in the doorway. She stared at him with wide, shocked eyes. Behind her, he saw Kemp Vanner holding his gun pressed to her spine.

"Come in, Belden," Vanner said lightly. "The lady has been hoping for your company. But give me your gun first. We don't want any accidents."

XVII

Vanner reached a hand around Molly. She licked her lips and bobbed her head, her eyes pleading with Clay.

Vanner said, "You might shoot me, Belden, but that wouldn't stop me from killing her before I died."

Clay put his gun in Vanner's hand and then stepped into the room as Vanner backed Molly out of the doorway. Clay said, "The rest of the town is gathering, Vanner. You haven't a chance. Get your men and ride out of here while you can."

"I thought you came to bargain," Vanner murmured. He smiled his cold smile. "By the time they get together and march to the judge's house, it will be too late, Belden. There won't be anything for them to save."

"There'll be tomorrow," Clay said.

"Tomorrow? What good will they be

then without leaders? Everyone in this town always looked to your precious Judge Lyles to tell him what to do! Without the judge, they'll look to someone else. To me!"

"And your men," Molly cried bitterly. "Those gunhands you brought in here! I should have known what you planned when I saw the first ones."

"But you were blinded by your pretty dresses and your shiny furniture, weren't you, my dear?" Vanner said cuttingly. He glanced at Clay. "Yes, me and my men. Don't you think they'll make a good police force, Belden?"

Clay put his back to the wall and studied the room. The bodies of Marnie and Pike had been removed from sight. There was nothing to indicate there had ever been a struggle in this room. Clay looked at the neat, well-kept furniture, at the tight, bright dress Molly Doane was wearing.

She met his gaze with hopeless eyes. She reached up automatically to tuck a strand of hair into place. Then her hand fell back to her side. Vanner moved away from her and dropped into a chair where he could keep his gun on her and watch Clay at the same time.

"You might as well relax, Belden. My

men know what they're doing. Your town friends won't be able to stop them."

It seemed to Clay that he could feel the seconds ticking away. He looked at Molly, seeking some sign of help there. But she stood rigid, dazed with the fear working inside her.

Clay said, "You helped me once tonight, Molly."

Her eyes focused on him. He moved his head in the direction of the fireplace a step to her right. She turned as he hoped she would, looking at the rack holding the poker.

Vanner said, "Move aside!" to Molly, and he leaned over to see what she was looking at.

Clay pushed himself away from the wall, forcing his sore leg to drive him the width of the room. He saw Vanner turn quickly back, moving with that swift, easy grace. He brought up his small gun and started out of the chair.

Clay left his feet as Vanner's gun cracked. Molly Doane screamed and the fireplace rack went over with a clatter as she tore the poker from it.

Vanner's bullet struck Clay's left shoulder, but the force of his dive carried him forward. He struck Vanner with his body, driving the smaller man back into the chair. It went over with a crash.

Vanner cried out in wild anger. He jerked his gun arm free and lashed out, raking Clay's face with the barrel. Clay's head went back and then he clamped his right arm on Vanner's gun wrist and rolled, pinning the gun to the floor. Pain blinded Clay and he fought through a murky red haze in an effort to get the gun away from Vanner. He got his hand on the gun and jerked, twisting free. He shook his head, clearing the blindness out of his eyes.

He heard the sodden thud of metal striking flesh. He turned to see Vanner's body stiffen and then jerk convulsively. His voice rose in a curse which broke off as he collapsed. His neat features were broken and torn where Molly Doane had smashed him with the poker.

She lifted it to strike again. Clay surged to his feet and caught her arm. "Stop it!" he said.

"I want to kill him!" she cried. "I want to kill him!"

Clay managed to take the poker from her and push her gently away from Vanner. "Let the law take care of that for you," he said.

He swayed dizzily and then caught himself. He found his gun and holstered it. He grabbed Vanner by the collar with his good hand and pulled him up.

Clay said to Molly, "Stay here!" and dragged Vanner out of the door and down the stairs. He put Vanner on his own horse and roped him into the saddle. Then, mounting the dun, Clay led Vanner's horse around the saloon and onto the main street.

He could see a knot of men moving ahead of him and he raced the dun away from the main street and into the alley. He had no time to answer questions now. He could feel the numbness wearing out of his shoulder and he knew he would have to hurry before the full pain from Vanner's bullet struck him.

He clenched his teeth and rode on. He could hear intermittent gunfire, and he felt a surge of relief. That meant those in the house were still holding out. He urged the dun to a faster pace.

Suddenly the sky lighted up in a great burst of flame. A shout rose and the firing picked up tempo. Clay saw that Tom Roddy's cottage had been set on fire, and he forced the dun into a straining gallop.

He reined in abruptly at the edge of the

light. He could see men crouched by the stable and behind the trees along the edge of the road that ran beside the house. Another half-dozen were coming from the front, hurrying from tree to tree. Torches flickered as men set them alight and moved into position from which they could charge the house.

Clay pulled Vanner's horse around and slapped it with his reins, sending it running into the middle of the judge's rear yard. He drew his gun and fired at a man breaking for the house, holding a flaming torch high. The man collapsed and his torch fell over in the dew-wet grass.

One wall of the cottage fell in, sending up a gout of flame. The firing from inside the house quickened as the light revealed the hiding places of the attakers.

A voice cried, "It's Vanner! He's tied! He's been caught!"

One of the men threw down his gun, turned and ran across the road away from the light. Then another man broke and another. Clay sent a quick shot after them, bringing them up short.

"Drop your guns and line up in the yard!" he called. He fired again as he saw a rifle swing in his direction. The rifleman clapped a hand to his arm and ran forward

193

to stand by Vanner's horse. Slowly, the others emerged from their hiding places, arms held high.

Clay saw Roy Ponders and Tom Roddy come onto the porch. He rode to the stairs leading up to the veranda and slid off the dun. "They're all yours, Sheriff, if you can find a jail big enough," he said.

He climbed the stairs slowly and went into the house. Through the shattered front windows he could see some of the men from town running for the back yard. Ponders would have deputies enough, Clay thought, as he walked to the sofa. He fell as he reached it, sprawling full length. He closed his eyes and let warm blackness enfold him.

Clay awakened to the sound of Doc Fraley's crab-apple voice. "No bones shattered," the doctor said tartly. "But keep him down and feed him good. He's got to build up blood. Lots of steak, that's what he needs."

"I know just what to do," Tonia said. "Beefsteak and potatoes."

Clay opened his eyes to see Tonia looking down at him. His face was sore where Vanner had raked it with his gun, and he winced when he tried to talk.

194

"How's your father?" he managed to ask.

"Better," Doc Fraley answered. "He needed a tonic. Next time I get a heart patient, I'll let him fight a lynch mob. Does wonders for the system!" He stalked out of the room.

Tonia's eyes laughed down at Clay. "Dad really is all right," she said. "And so are you. So stop frowning like that."

Clay said, "I was thinking about the judge's cattle up in the mountains."

"He's already hired men to bring them down," she said. "Now be quiet."

"About Molly Doane," Clay said. "She —"

"She's buying the saloon from Damson's estate for a dollar and other considerations," Tonia said. "Dad isn't a lawyer and a judge for nothing, you know."

She put her face close to his and frowned. "Now will you be quiet?"

Clay said, "I had to get those things off my mind to leave thinking room for something more important." He smiled lopsidedly at her. "But with nothing to concern me until spring, I guess I don't have to think about that for a while yet after all. I —"

His voice stopped as Tonia leaned forward and silenced him with her lips. She straightened up. "I've waited five years," she said. "And I'm not going to wait any longer. So you'd better start thinking about *that* right now!"

"All right," Clay said with a wide grin. "Bring me that steak the doc ordered."

CANLEY

We hope you have enjoyed this Large Print book. Other Thorndike, Wheeler or Chivers Press Large Print books are available at your library or directly from the publishers.

For more information about current and up-coming titles, please call or write, without obligation, to:

Publisher
Thorndike Press
295 Kennedy Memorial Drive
Waterville, ME   04901
Tel. (800) 223-1244

Or visit our Web site at:
www.gale.com/thorndike
www.gale.com/wheeler

OR

Chivers Large Print
published by BBC Audiobooks Ltd
St James House, The Square
Lower Bristol Road
Bath BA2 3BH
England
Tel. +44(0) 800 136919
email: bbcaudiobooks@bbc.co.uk
www.bbcaudiobooks.co.uk

All our Large Print titles are designed for easy reading, and all our books are made to last.